Sylvie Germain

Invitation to a Journey

Éclats de sel

Translated from the French by
Christine Donougher

Dedalus

Dedalus would like to thank The Arts Council of England, The Burgess Programme of the French Ministry of Foreign Affairs and The French Ministry of Culture in Paris for their assistance in producing this book.

Published in the UK by Dedalus Ltd, Langford Lodge, St Judith's Lane, Sawtry, Cambs, PE28 5XE
email: DedalusLimited@compuserve.com
web site: www.dedalusbooks.com

ISBN 1 903517 16 8

Dedalus is distributed in the United States by SCB Distributors, 15608 South New Century Drive, Gardena, California 90248
email: info@scbdistributors.com
web site: www.scbdistributors.com

Dedalus is distributed in Australia & New Zealand by Peribo Pty Ltd, 58 Beaumont Road, Mount Kuring-gai, N.S.W. 2080
email: peribo@bigpond.com

Dedalus is distributed in Canada by Marginal Distribution, Unit 102, 277 George Street North, Peterborough, Ontario, KJ9 3G9
email: marginal@marginalbook.com
web site: www.marginal.com

Publishing History
First published in France in 1996
First Dedalus edition in 2003

Typeset by RefineCatch Limited, Bungay, Suffolk
Printed in Finland by WS Bookwell

A C.I.P. listing for this book is available on request.

institut français

French Literature from Dedalus

French Language Literature in translation is an important part of Dedalus's list, with French being the language *par excellence* of literary fantasy.

The Land of Darkness – Daniel Arsand £8.99
Séraphita – Balzac £6.99
The Quest of the Absolute – Balzac £6.99
The Experience of the Night – Marcel Béalu £8.99
Episodes of Vathek – Beckford £6.99
The Devil in Love – Jacques Cazotte £5.99
Les Diaboliques – Barbey D'Aurevilly £7.99
Milagrosa – Mercedes Deambrosis £8.99
The Man in Flames – Serge Filippini £10.99
Spirite (and Coffee Pot) – Théophile Gautier £6.99
Angels of Perversity – Rémy de Gourmont £6.99
The Book of Nights – Sylvie Germain £8.99
The Book of Tobias – Sylvie Germain £7.99
Night of Amber – Sylvie Germain £8.99
Days of Anger – Sylvie Germain £8.99
The Medusa Child – Sylvie Germain £8.99
The Weeping Woman – Sylvie Germain £6.99
Infinite Possibilities – Sylvie Germain £8.99
Invitation to a Journey – Sylvie Germain £7.99
Là-Bas – J. K. Huysmans £7.99
En Route – J. K. Huysmans £7.99
The Cathedral – J. K. Huysmans £7.99
The Oblate of St Benedict – J. K. Huysmans £7.99
The Mystery of the Yellow Room – Gaston Leroux £7.99
The Perfume of the Lady in Black – Gaston Leroux £8.99

Monsieur de Phocas – Jean Lorrain £8.99
The Woman and the Puppet – Pierre Louÿs £6.99
Portrait of an Englishman in his Chateau – Pieyre de Mandiargues £7.99
Abbé Jules – Octave Mirbeau £8.99
Le Calvaire – Octave Mirbeau £7.99
The Diary of a Chambermaid – Octave Mirbeau £7.99
Sébastien Roch – Octave Mirbeau £9.99
Torture Garden – Octave Mirbeau £7.99
Smarra & Trilby – Charles Nodier £6.99
Manon Lescaut – Abbé Prévost £7.99
Tales from the Saragossa Manuscript – Jan Potocki £5.99
Monsieur Venus – Rachilde £6.99
The Marquise de Sade – Rachilde £8.99
Enigma – Rezvani £8.99
The Wandering Jew – Eugene Sue £10.99
Micromegas – Voltaire £4.95

Anthologies featuring French Literature in translation:

The Dedalus Book of French Horror: the 19c – ed T. Hale £9.99
The Dedalus Book of Decadence – ed Brian Stableford £7.99
The Dedalus Book of Surrealism – ed Michael Richardson £9.99
Myth of the World: Surrealism 2 – ed Michael Richardson £9.99
The Dedalus Book of Medieval Literature – ed Brian Murdoch £9.99
The Dedalus Book of Sexual Ambiguity – ed Emma Wilson £8.99
The Decadent Cookbook – Medlar Lucan & Durian Gray £9.99
The Decadent Gardener – Medlar Lucan & Durian Gray £9.99

THE AUTHOR

Sylvie Germain is the author of ten works of fiction, eight of which have been published by Dedalus, a study of the painter Vermeer and a religious meditation. Her work has been translated into seventeen languages and has received worldwide acclaim.

Sylvie Germain's first novel *The Book of Nights* was published in France in 1985 and received instant recognition. It has won five literary prizes as well as the T.L.S. Scott Moncrieff Translation Prize in England. The novel's story is continued in *Night of Amber* in 1987. Her third novel, *Days of Anger*, won the Prix Femina in 1989. It was followed by *The Medusa Child* in 1991 and *The Weeping Woman on the Streets of Prague* in 1992, the beginning of her Prague trilogy, continued with *Infinite Possibilities* in 1993 and then *Invitation to a Journey* in 1996. *The Book of Tobias* (1999) saw a return to a rural French setting and *la France profonde.*

Dedalus will publish Sylvie Germain's latest novel *Chanson des Mal-Aimants* in the autumn of 2004

THE TRANSLATOR

Christine Donougher read English and French at Cambridge and after a career in publishing, is now a freelance translator and editor.

Her many translations from French and Italian include Sylvie Germain's novels *Days of Anger*, *Night of Amber* and *The Book of Tobias* and Giovanni Verga's *Sparrow* and *Temptation (and other stories)*.

Her translation of Sylvie Germain's *The Book of Nights* won the T.L.S. Scott Moncrieff Prize for the best translation of a Twentieth Century French Novel during 1992.

To Lubomír Marinék

Which of us has not, consciously or unconsciously, succumbed to mystification? Which of us has not paid them often exorbitant tribute? Could not a work be written on 'mystification as one of the fine arts'? What of history, for that matter? And claims to fame? Let us experiment: let us reverse the headlines on a number of articles in the newspaper, or swop the photographs round, leaving the captions as they are. Maybe this would cheer us up, maybe not. Man attains knowledge by strange routes.

Jirí Kolár

PREFACE

A solitary beech stood there in the middle of a flat landscape beneath a sky of swirling shades of slate and lavender. It stood very erect in the heart of this twofold immensity of open ground and cold light, this twofold barrenness, and it bore its globe-like crest, the colour of amber and rust, very high in the blue silence. A beech in sober majesty, conversing with the wind, the emptiness, its own shadow, the waning light.

It was a dreary place, and yet extraordinary. Devoid of relief, chromatically impoverished, a vast sky, an austere and low-drawn line of horizon. But there was the tree, with its ashen trunk, like a gash in the dull blue of the sky, the rounded shape of its boughs like a challenge to such levelness, its coppery foliage like a gong harbouring obscure resonances. There was this beech, posted like a sentry in the twilight, with the sturdiness of a long-enduring body, in waiting. It occupied space with simplicity, with power, entirely concentrated on itself, its invisible tree heart, its inaudible tree song, its arboreal solitude. It occupied time with tenacity, with patience, endlessly weaving dreams beneath its grey bark, twisting and twining the woody threads of its age-old memory.

But the beech was suddenly wrested from its immobility and began slowly to glide across the sky until it was lost from view. Was it going to rejoin the forests? Was it abandoning its excessive solitude? Was it drifting off in the current of a dream that had sprung up on the horizon, in the swell of the clouds, or was it fleeing to keep a secret that its rusty leaves were beginning to cast abroad. In any case, it disappeared; the barrenness of the place was then at its most overwhelming, the blueness of the evening seemed darker, the earth more desolate. Ludvik felt a little distressed as he saw the tree grow distant, although at the same time he sighed with relief – after more than twenty minutes stopped in open countryside the train was finally moving off again. Ludvik picked up the art magazine he had laid down on the tabletop; it opened of its own accord at a page that was all crinkled from having had coffee spilt on it. Dark brown stains spattered the lines of an article devoted to Leonardo da Vinci's 'Last Supper'. Ludvik read the caffeinated text and found a taste of bitter irony to it. It was about the fresco's disastrous state of conservation and about the work that had been undertaken to try to save it; the author traced the history of this damage to which certain incompetent restorers, if not charlatans, had regrettably contributed in the past. Since the beginning of his journey Ludvik had been dwelling on nothing but gloomy thoughts, all relating to the idea of decay, both physical and mental. This story about the ruining of a masterpiece affected him like a finger on a wound.

A second article examined the structure of the 'Last Supper', and analysed the dynamic of the poses and gestures of the figures; this article was illustrated with reproductions, particularly with details of the hands. Those of Christ, held apart, marking a central space, and those of the disciples, of such expressivity that they seemed to speak, wondering, exclaiming, calling to each other, seeking to understand, weighing the moment. A moment of tragic weight, because fraught with the disclosure the Master has just made to his apostles: one of them is going to betray him. The detail of the hands of the one to whom it has fallen to carry out the dark deed of this betrayal is included in the iconography. In contrast with the hands of the eleven true disciples, which are so lively and animated, those of Judas look unwieldy, tense, especially the right hand, clasped round the purse filled with the fateful coins. And with this encumbered hand he has, without realizing it, just overturned a salt cellar, whose contents spill across the tablecloth. Judas, the one who breaks the covenant, refuses to become the salt of the earth. Ludvik yawned and closed the magazine, which he laid on the tabletop.

The train was now travelling through fields made indistinct by an ever denser mist, while the sky turned brown, faintly veined with trails of pink that blurred the line of the horizon. The landscape dissolved in an ochre gloom and the few trees that lined the embankment lacked the powerfulness of the beech that by its sole presence had made the space around it a disturbing and solemn setting. There was something haggard, wretched, about those stunted trees shivering in the mist. Ludvik felt himself shudder from the same damp cold as that which caused those trees to shudder. Truly, this hour of day exuded only ugliness and sadness, and held no promise of any brightness. This dusk was bleak and disheartening, and Ludvik, in unison with it, was glum and disheartened.

He was returning home from the town of T, where he had been to visit one of his former teachers, Joachym Brum – everyone used to call him the great Brum. There was a time, in his youth, when Ludvik had felt such keen admiration for this man whom he had regarded as a second father, an obliquely related father who had brought him into the world more fully, or at least in a different way. Then, as the years passed, the bonds of this oblique relationship slowly slackened, even frayed away. Ludvik had gone off to explore areas of thought other than those in which Brum roamed with perseverance and quiet fervour. And Brum himself had gradually faded into a character of golden legend, a legend whose gilt had faded, then cracked.

Joachym Brum had been a nomad, one of that race of sedentary nomads, those for whom the least flower blossoms into a garden, a drop of water contains a river, the quivering of a shadow or a gleam of light on a wall becomes an invitation to dream; those for whom a painting is a landscape of limitless expanse and abounding views, and words, words above all, are miracles of space, movement, echoes. Brum had been surveying the geography of language, of images and forms all his life; he had learned how high and arid are the true terrains of language and those of the visible world. Brum had learned several different languages, the better to explore these high-altitude terrains in their acoustic diversity, their variation of light. He often said, it was not the paths leading elsewhere that mattered, only that there should be an elsewhere rooted in the plenitude of desire, extending interminably to the heart's horizon. And so he had spent his life travelling quietly in the silence of his living-room.

For a few years he had guided Ludvik through this silence with its infinite murmur of rhymes and rhythms. And when Ludvik had allowed himself to be overcome by the dizzying effect of those verbal heights, confusing rigour and preciosity, Brum was able to correct him. One day when Ludvik submitted to him some very obscure and ill-conceived poems of his own, Brum had by way of comment quoted a few lines by Cyprian Kamil Norwid:

'You say: "My song is a song of love . . ."
Do you think you can deceive me?
I don't hear the chords vibrate beneath your fingers.
You're just a printer of poems.'

Then, still citing Norwid, he had added:

'Learn to give words their primary meaning,
All the mystery that lies in perception:
Rhymes? They are in the lines, not at the end of them.
Stars are not where they shine.'

It was impossible to recall a conversation with Brum without immediately evoking verses, phrases, aphorisms quoted from some author or other, for Brum was remarkable for the way he was always quoting from memory. He had to such an extent made language his territory, without frontiers or a capital, that he moved with equal freedom in whichever region he passed through, and was supremely at home in whichever word-place he dwelt a while. A walking library of talking books that always opened at the right page, to suit the moment and the person to whom he was talking.

'All the mystery that lies in perception.' As far as Ludvik was concerned, mystery had long since been missing from the perception of things, of people, of the world. And at this grey and sluggish time of day, in this compartment reeking of grime and tobacco, on this lurching train as it rattled through dreary fields bounded by bushes that looked like chilly spectres, there was less glimmer than ever of this mystery, and he felt merely oppressed by a sense of boredom, pointlessness, clammy absurdity. All of Brum's magic could not suffice any more to dispel such disenchantment. No poem, however wonderful, was now capable of saving Ludvik from his apathy, of imposing silence on the deep and yawning emptiness ever expanding inside him. Ludvik had sunk too far into a state of inner destitution.

But in any case there was nothing left of Brum's magic. The old man Ludvik had just left was no more than a simulacrum of Brum the nomad; he no longer roamed amid the beauties of elsewhere, he now wandered aimlessly in tiny circles in a wasteland.

The vast geographies of thought and memory that he had so magnificently explored were devastated, strewn with wildernesses and pitfalls. Old Brum's memory was more pitted and desolate than the craters of the moon. He could hardly speak any more, stumbling over words, mumbling incoherent, incongruous sounds, somewhat like Hölderlin confined by madness to Carpenter Zimmer's house, and only managing to stammer out words of uncertain meaning, like that seesaw utterance 'Pallaksch', which meant sometimes yes, sometimes no, both yes and no, neither yes nor no. Pallaksch, Pallaksch – old age was sabotaging the great Brum's memory, old age was playing havoc with his thinking and his dreams, making all books obsolete.

It was all very well Ludvik feeling pity for this devastation, but it did no good, it was of no help to old Brum and his drifting mind. What would have been needed to save Joachym Brum from his decrepitude, or at least to allay his distress, was pity illuminated by pure love, patience, self-denial. Ludvik knew he was incapable of such love, or rather too bruised to risk getting too deeply involved in caring about another person. Ludvik lacked that impetuosity, that inexhaustible generosity that only self-forgetfulness affords. The more profound the forgetfulness, the more lavish the heart.

A few drops of rain formed beads on the windowpane and soon trickled across the glass in oblique lines. It was almost dark. Ludvik finally got up to switch on the ceiling light, which flickered for a long while before casting an acerbic glare. Pallaksch, Pallaksch, the train swayed on the rails. Ludvik's thoughts kept returning to old Brum. True, old age was ugly, and so sneakingly cruel. That smell of rancidness and urine that Brum's clothes gave off, that humiliating smell was as painful to Ludvik as the old man's incoherent mumblings. This dual disintegration, of body and mind, tormented him. Would he too one day be afflicted with this humiliation? He wondered which was the more grievous pain: seeing the image of those you love and admire degenerate, or seeing your own image defiled in the eyes of others? Sometimes the two distorted perceptions converge and exacerbate each other, as in the case of love or friendship scorned, when the other turns traitor. The image of yourself is then so ill-favoured by the deserting party that you are suddenly overcome with unforgiving lucidity about yourself. A lucidity that is all the harsher because it comes too late, and all the more unreasonable because of its desperation. The entire past is reviewed under a hyper-powerful magnifying glass; the lies, the ignoble behaviour, the shabbiness of the betrayer are hunted out, and their odiousness exaggerated. And so there are two of you observing each other through the wrong end of the telescope, mutually belittling each other and reducing each other to caricatures. The traducing of love is then at its peak, and the heart at its most irresolute.

Perhaps the worst thing about this grotesque game of diminishing and tarnishing each other's image is the way the image of yourself in your own eyes is blighted, when you catch yourself acting, or even thinking, like those whose behaviour you condemned, whose opinions you despised. Then your loathing turns against you, and you lose your self-respect, disappointed, and even appalled, to discover you are so undistinguished. It is then extremely difficult from this nadir in being thus mirrored to regard others with any admiration or pity. The lame and mangy dog that whines in your heart is incapable of anything but exposing the underlying meanness and vanity in everything and everyone. Even in Eva, Brum's niece, who devoted herself to her uncle with such forbearance, Ludvik could not help detecting hints of dullness. Like an ailing plant, she had grafted her life on to her uncle's, acting as his servant, companion and secretary, and now as a sister of charity. Time seemed to have no hold on her. Ludvik had always known her as a tall, slim woman, even quite skinny, quietly moving about the rooms of that apartment with its invariably gleaming floor, furniture and windowpanes, and she herself looked like a shiny cloth, from all the washing, scrubbing and polishing she did. But oddly, this shininess made her seem lacklustre. A woman, all bone and silence, continuously engaged, slowly and solemnly, in household chores. A woman of indeterminate age, drab and colourless, whose goodness had the hollow ring of a heart resigned to everyday's sameness.

Yet in his youth, when he was one of Brum's students, he had a brief liaison with Eva – flirting with the niece who lived under the same roof was a way of claiming a little intimacy with the great Brum. Their affair ended abruptly, because of Eva. One fine day she just gave him the brush-off, turned cool, if not icy, towards him, without any warning or the least explanation. This hardly had any effect on Ludvik, who in the course of their chaste romance did not give up philandering with other girls on the side, nor did he try to find out the reasons for this abrupt, and definitive, cooling of sentiment in Eva, who did not even deign to shake his hand any more. All that was so long ago, Ludvik had retained no memory of it. And when he saw her again, the previous day, after more than eleven years, he felt no emotion whatsoever. Only amazement, to find her so little changed, whereas Brum was scarcely recognizable, and had grown so pathetic. It was as though the years that seemed to have glanced off Eva – just touching her hair, which was greying a little at the temples – had only affected Brum, doubly ravaging and ruining him.

Pallaksch, Pallaksch, the train travelled on in the darkness, through the rain. This journey was endless. It was life, crawling along, getting bogged down. Ludvik felt the same sense of disgust that had made him flee his country eleven years ago. An exile without heroism or romanticism. It was concern for his mental health that made Ludvik decide one day to emigrate. This plan had been gestating for a long time inside him, but in a vague way, and suddenly, just as an illness breaks out after a long period of incubation, the intention became a matter of urgency. This was triggered, in Marianske Lazne, one mild autumn afternoon, when he happened to be there visiting a relative who was taking the waters.

It was a long time since the glorious days when those taking the waters were crowned heads – whether their crowns were royal, or imperial, or of laurel, woven by the muses of poetry and music – who came to cure their hepatic languidness and heartaches to the sound of violins and welling springs. There, one got drunk on bubbly water, romance and amorous excitement, delicate lungs breathed deeply of the healthy fragrance of conifers circling the pretty colonnaded villa with its onion domes, fountains and gilded stucco, and one fainted away with passions as melancholy as they were voluptuous. Of that superlative age nothing survived but a rather delapidated decor. All that remained unchanged, and continued to be faithfully observed, was Goethe's wise counsel, given by one who knew full well what he was talking about, never to go to a spa town without taking the precaution of falling in love, at the risk of dying of boredom. Young privates allowed out of their barracks would walk up and down the street, awkwardly holding hands with some fresh-faced silly goose wearing an ugly dress she'd bought at the Co-op; pot-bellied sixty-year-old couples would coo in park avenues, absolutely thrilled to be once more savouring the delights of adulterous love; beneath the arches, glum musicians would play medleys of syrupy tunes in front of an audience of old ladies bobbing their heads the better to immerse themselves in the melodies, occasionally breaking off to raise to their lips their china cups full of fizzy water of therapeutic virtues. Everyone forestalled boredom as best as they could, for as long as they could, but it always prevailed, no one got the better of it. It eroded the façades of the houses, consumed hearts, corroded the air and the light. Strolling along the streets and in the parks where so many couples of all ages dallied, Ludvik had been struck by the vacancy of people's faces with their foolish smiles devoid of any joyfulness, their expressionless eyes glazed with somnolence. Hold hands as they might, or encircle each other's waist, or shoulders, their hearts were not in it, their hearts could not find it in themselves to flutter, to thrill, to be gladdened. Their hearts were aching with emptiness and dullness.

Late in the afternoon, Ludvik passed by a hotel situated just outside town. Long tables and wooden benches had been set up in the garden, garishly coloured lanterns swung from wires hung over tables awash with beer, a crackling loudspeaker poured out music so crass and unctuous it put one in mind of a trickle of lard. And beneath the citric- and tomato-coloured lanterns, in the evening air rank with the smell of beer and sausages, dancers nostalgic for their long-departed youth shuffled to the sound of these lubricious dronings. They swayed about like seals tossed in the surge, the slimy surge of those cheap sentimental songs, and those seated round them appplauded these ungainly dance-hall veterans with loud bangings of their beer mugs. A couple who had danced longer and more clumsily than the rest received a thunderous ovation; then these heros of the dance floor, breathless and flattered, acknowledged their public by bowing their heads in all directions, and returned to one of the tables, their steps unsure. And it was at that moment that Ludvik, who was leaning over the garden fence watching the festivities, noticed these two dancers were blind. Their eyes were glassy and their movements uncertain. This realization caused a short circuit in Ludvik's mind: this couple of oafs who had been clodhopping about without being able to see anything around them, cavorting in beery darkness to the sound of tacky music, while in the distance the mountains glowed red in the sunset and the birds gave out their fluty songs on the edge of the forests, this somnambulant couple appeared to him as the very incarnation of the malady that afflicted his country – a debility of taste and mind, an anemia of the heart, a blindness of the soul. The ruling mediocracy had inoculated people with this illness, taking care to keep them cooped up inside tightly-closed frontiers so as to contaminate as many of them as possible. This couple were the paradigm of the model citizen: crippled in their freedom, replete with deceit and lies, and happy to be so. Ludvik drew himself up behind the fence, turned on his heels, and briskly walked straight back to town. As he walked, he made up his mind: he was going to emigrate, he had to, and as quickly as possible. And that is what he did, the following month.

Pallaksch, Pallaksch, the train travelled on in the darkness, through the rain. This journey was like his life, which was crawling along, getting bogged down. Ludvik felt a sense of disgust even greater than that which in the past made him flee his country. For now the malady was inside him, reversed of course, but just as insiduous and sclerotic in its effect; he was replete with liberty, but crippled in ideals, and bitterly dissatisfied with being so. During those eleven years spent abroad, he had travelled a great deal, had various different kinds of jobs, met loads of people, made a few friends, had several love affairs, one of them so overwhelming, so passionate, it eclipsed all the others; it dazzled him, then left him stripped naked, flayed alive, completely helpless.

Several months after Esther had sent him packing, he saw her again one day, by chance. It was in a metro station, he was standing on an escalator going up, she on one coming down. There were too many people packed in front of him and behind for him to escape. But even if the place had been deserted, he would have remained petrified where he stood. The moment he saw her, before there was time for any thought to come into his mind, he felt a violent instinct to vomit and everything inside his body seemed to heave. Suddenly he was no longer in control of himself, and especially not of his eyes. He could not take them off her. She confronted him like a ghost. Despite her small size, she dominated the crowd. Despite her ordinary coat and altogether unexceptional manner, she looked absurdly, compellingly, majestic. Her Beloved Majesty, Her Most Unfaithful Majesty. She descended towards him, and there was no one else but her, the entire mass of humanity around her and around him was the colour of ashes, insignificant to the point of being transparent. She descended towards him, bore down on him, cut to his heart, and shattered everything, though she did not move. She descended within him, to the depths of his madness. And he rose, hypnotized, towards the blind wall of her slightly averted face, towards the white darkness of her eyes that did not see him, towards her fallow-lying heart that did not even sense his presence, detecting nothing. He was on the shelf, rejected, already forgotten, and he still loved her, in defiance of everything, in defiance of his own will, pride and reason, and he felt mortified that he had the insanity to love her still, even amid the disgust, anger and scorn she now inspired in him. He rose like a condemned man, mindless with panic and grief, towards that forevermore untouchable woman. He rose, in free-fall, into love's desolation.

Then he decided he must go, move away from that town, though he had made his home there for several years. He did not want to risk another encounter with this woman who still had such dreadful power over him. He did not want to become the poodle of a spectre, the slave of a lost illusion. So once again, it was for health reasons, his psychological and emotional health, that he took flight. What followed was an exile in reverse, since in the meantime his country had opened its borders and cleaned up the atmosphere. But it is not so easy to go back to square one, especially when it is not in the same place any more, when it has acquired a new look, and done so in too much haste and too much for show, swopping party rule, with its woodenness of expression and art of lying, for the rule of money, with its saccharine lingua franca and art of deception. Back in his home town, which was continuously overrun by hordes of tourists, swarming with businessmen, where college drop-outs full of artistic ambitions gathered on its fringes and arrivistes of every kind performed their social gymnastics, while the local population, not yet accustomed to this new pace, dawdled, Ludvik had to start again more or less from scratch. He did not complain, he had had plenty of practice in living from hand to mouth. Anyway, he was not the kind of man to complain or protest, he was far too indifferent to everything, indifferent to himself. He scraped a living, from translations and articles, saw a few friends, and contented himself with one-night stands when the opportunity arose.

So he had come home, but only in outward appearance. At heart, he had never escaped from that desolation of love into which he had tumbled. And it was not just a matter of passion, which eventually, with the passage of time, you are prepared to mourn; but a much vaster desolation, of love for others, for yourself, for life, a desolation of tenderness and compassion. There was no longer any feeling or enthusiasm in him, no capacity for wonder and desire, nothing but curiosity, which remained keen, by natural disposition and force of habit. But a very fragmented, superficial and fickle curiosity. So he veered from one focus of interest to another, from one anecdote to another; he could only tolerate people in homeopathic doses, and life in fits and starts. He was in every sphere one who favoured brevity. But in between bursts of energy he sank back into melancholy.

That evening, everything conspired to bring to a pitch the basso continuo of his lassitude; this puffing train, this relentless rain. And he felt aged by Brum's old age, stricken, by an obscure ricochet effect, in some unlocatable but painful part of his being. He suddenly gave such a big yawn of dejection that his eyes filled with tears. He rose and went out into the corridor to stretch his legs. When he returned to his seat, he discovered that during his absence a passenger had settled down on the seat opposite him. This presence vexed him, he was not in the mood to engage in conversation, nor even to put up with any company whatsoever. But the intruder paid no attention to him. He sat very upright, well back in his seat, with his arms crossed, his face turned to the window. Ludvik picked up his magazine again, which persisted in opening at the same page; he turned the pages, in annoyance, and began reading another article, but was unable to concentrate.

The passenger continued to contemplate the night-darkened window. Ludvik, whose distracted gaze wandered from his magazine to the window, noticed that the man was surreptiously observing him, indirectly, in the reflection of his face on the glass. He did likewise, concealing his indiscretion with cigarette smoke. But in this game of smoked mirrors, the passenger's face remained a blur. All that Ludvik could see was a faint profile of pale ochre against a dark background streaked with rain. Yet something about the little that he did manage to discern intrigued him, although he was unable to recall the person of whom it reminded him. He did not go on racking his brains for long because he soon grew drowsy, so lulling was the swaying of the train and the beating of the rain on the window. His head nodded on to his chest and he fell asleep. This doze actually lasted only a short time, but long enough to be disturbed by a dream consisting of fragments of memories and impressions.

He is walking through his home town, but the town is altered, there is something odd about the architecture, because buildings from other towns are mixed in among the local buildings, without rhyme or reason. So, the keep of a fortified castle in the region of T rises in the distance on the hill of Vysehrad in place of the two towers of the church of SS Peter and Paul; the ruins of the synagogue in Berlin are adjacent to the church of St Nicholas; the Certovka Reach is dry, with piles of scrap iron, and old cars in it; statues like those round the basin of the Latone fountain at Versailles grin from the parapet of the Charles Bridge, which, suddenly reduced to a wooden walkway, leads directly to a suburb of the town, over towards Vrsovice.

Ludvik is walking down a street lined with houses built all crookedly. This peculiar street looks derelict, the façades about to collapse. Yet all this chaos remains standing, as though welded in place by the intensely dark frosty night that lacquers the sky and the walls. It is raining, but this rain does not wet anything. A dry heavy sleet is falling, which makes a sound like a spinet as it hits the ground and the roofs. This haunting music carries through the entire neighbourhood whose empty streets are very resonant.

He enters a café, as if the music had suddenly driven him inside. He goes down a few steps, comes into a huge low-ceilinged room so smoky it is hard to make out what is going on, or even if anyone is there. In one corner, however, he notices an inordinately long billiard table, whose cloth looks green with the shimmering of mud and duckweed. He seems to glimpse through the smoky haze the figures of a few players equipped with cues that have a silvery glint. When they lean over the table to aim for a ball that does not exist, a little light is cast on their faces by the reflection of the green-water cloth. They have the faces of frogs, those of the statues round the Latone fountain; they stare with bulging eyes and open wide their batrachian mouths, wagging their heads.

He is sitting at a dark wooden table with glistening beer rings on it. Opposite him is a man half-hidden behind an ancient typewriter. This fellow, bent over the keyboard, keeps tapping away, with no less obstination than clumsiness; the staccato sound of the keys is the same as that of the dry sleet. These hammering sounds drive invisible nails into him that pin him to his chair. The guy now and then darts interrogating glances at him, as if he were taking down a deposition. After a while Ludvik becomes irritated and exclaims: 'But now what can you possibly be writing? You haven't asked me any questions and I haven't told you anything!' Then the man shouts at him, 'What a man doesn't say is the salt of conversation!' And with that, he suddenly stands up, whinnying and stamping his hoofs on the ground, for Ludvik now discovers that the lower half of this individual's body is that of a horse. And the typing centaur goes bucking round the table, while continuing to whinny in a piercing voice, and as he leaves he lashes Ludvik's face with a stinging whip of his tail.

Ludvik woke with a start. Caught in a draft, the window curtain was flapping in his face. The train had just stopped at a station the name of which he could not read because his carriage was too far down the platform. The passenger must have got off, the compartment was empty again. The journey took another hour and finally they were at the terminus. Ludvik stood up to collect his bag and his raincoat. When he took the coat from the rack where he had put it, and unfolded it, he realized it was not his. The make, size, shape and colour were the same, but the condition it was in was not at all the same. This twin raincoat was all creased, worn to a shine at the elbows, the collar and cuffs were threadbare, there were buttons missing, the hem had come half unsewn, the lining was full of tears, and the whole thing was extremely grubby. And to add a touch of derisory elegance to this scarecrow's rag, there was a stalk of saltwort in the buttonhole. Ludvik immediately suspected the passenger who had got off an hour earlier, and he wondered if that strange character had exchanged this shabby raincoat for his deliberately or inadvertently. Either way, Ludvik did very badly out of it and he cursed the stranger. He searched the pockets, which had holes in the bottom of them of course, then inspected the inside chest pocket. From this he extracted a little glass jar containing a few greyish crystals. Written on a tiny label stuck on the lid was the name of the Wieliczka salt-mine. 'What a great find this is,' grumbled Ludvik opening the jar and pouring the glittering salt gems into his palm, 'diamonds still in the making! This journey has really been too salty for words!' He threw the crystals on to the floor, the jar into the rubbish bin, and continued his search, but found no papers, no other object, no clue of any kind in the raincoat, which he left on the seat.

It was only as he was coming out of the station that he remembered that in a pocket of his lost gabardine he had left an envelope that Eva had given him just as he was leaving, after he had said good-bye to old Brum, whose trembling hand he had shaken. A fat brown envelope containing a medium-sized notebook.

'Here, this is for you,' she said when he was already on the doorstep. 'It's a book in which Joachym jotted down notes, ideas, as they came to him. A kind of scrapbook of texts or works that he planned to write. He won't be needing it any more.'

'What about you? Don't you want to keep it?' Ludvik asked.

'No, there are still plenty other notebooks, papers, publications . . . take it as a reminder of him.'

He slipped the envelope into his pocket and forgot to open it on the train; or rather he felt so uncomfortable thinking about the haggard old man whom he had just left, that he put off reading the notebook until later, and preferred to flick through his art magazine. But now the notebook was lost, and he was far more upset about this loss than that of his raincoat. He veered between regret, anger – as much against the passenger on the train as himself – and shame. For once Eva had shown some trust in him, he had immediately proved himself unworthy of it. He went straight home, chilled to the bone, in a filthy mood.

FACE TO FACE

At about midday the next day, Ludvik went into the Oural Inn for a quick lunch. As he was eating a pork stew and cabbage salad he thought about Brum, and old age, when the curtain comes down with such cruel slowness and humiliation. 'Death snatches the living, but without carrying him off completely. Spirits of the dead caught in a time warp . . .' he said to himself, shaking the saltcellar over his plate. It was empty. He sprinkled a pinch of paprika instead. At that moment a group of seven workers arrived, who installed themselves round the table where he was sitting. They were talking loudly, but Ludvik paid no attention to what they were saying. He continued to ponder on old age. As he reached towards the bread basket, one of his table companions made exactly the same move, and their fingers came into contact on the surface of a roll encrusted with grains of coarse salt. Ludvik immediately withdrew his hand. The other fellow then pushed the basket towards him and waited for him to help himself. He was a young man, rather slight in stature, dressed in oil-stained overalls, like his companions. He had a long bony face, and tow-like ash-blond hair, tied back at the nape of his neck in a pony tail. He had a downy fuzz on his chin, and wore a silver ring in his left ear. The fellow sitting next to him had tattooed arms.

Having swallowed his last mouthful, Ludvik called

the waitress over to pay. One of the coins she gave back to him rolled across the table until it was stopped by the mug of beer belonging to the young worker. He picked up the coin with his bony fingers and spun it round. It went reeling among the bread-crumbs and grains of coarse salt that had fallen on the tablecloth, but weirdly did not topple over. With a flick of his fingernail, the young man increased its momentum, and the coin began to spin round with an equilibrium as unsteady as it was obstinate. It twirled among the cutlery and beer mugs, a tiny metal will-o'-the-wisp, iridescent with a light whose source Ludvik could not determine. After much zigzagging it came to rest in front of him.

'Heads,' said the young man in a toneless voice. The coin had indeed fallen face up. Then he added, 'I'd have betted on it. What about you?'

Ludvik gazed in confusion at the youth impassively observing him. 'Betted on what?' he asked.

The young man did not respond, but his companions all shrugged their shoulders in unison, their upturned hands held apart, and remained momentarily frozen in this dubious attitude. They all had fingernails ringed with dirt, and it looked good to Ludvik, all these men with their hands raised to the same height, in a gesture of uncertainty and derision. Then slowly they let their arms drop. The young man was still staring at him with his distant gaze, devoid of expression. His eyes were so pale, a washed-out, almost transparent blue, that their irises seemed to be fashioned from a block of salt, and Ludvik suddenly had the impression that all the tiny grains scattered over the tablecloth were glints of his saline gaze that had rained in fine drops from between his blond eyelashes. An absurd idea crossed his mind. 'This young man has the tears of a seabird, which he sprinkles over his companions' blackened fingernails.' But soon the insistence of that diaphanous gaze and the silence reigning over the table made him feel uncomfortable. He automatically pocketed the coin, got up and left.

He took the tram to go back to the centre, but it was such a lovely day that he got off halfway to continue the journey on foot. The town exulted in purple, coral, bright orange and amber yellow; the roofs and domes were at one with the trees stripped bare by the wind, casting into the air, into the sky and the streets, hosts of flame-leaves, of red-gold flakes, that whirled about, sometimes friskily, sometimes listlessly, depending on how the wind blew. It was October sowing-time, and while walking through these flurries Ludvik was thinking that trees died with far more panache than men did. But interrupting and suspending his train of thought, the image of the workers, shrugging their shoulders and raising their dirty fingernailed hands with a look of bafflement, suddenly burst upon him.

He went to the House of the Stone Bell where there was an exhibition of Jiri Kolar. He lingered for a moment in front of the glass cases displaying the poem-objects; curious poems, in three dimension, in relief, in colour. Sedimentary poem-images composed of strata, of tucks and folds, like the memory, the heart, thoughts and dreams. Orogenic poems, genealogical images, but whose layers of earth defy chronological order, and whose roots intermingle in every direction. Then he studied the collages, visions of the town in convulsion, with distorted façades, broken roofs and towers, tangling with the clouds, tipsy churches incapable of standing upright, and writhing with laughter or doubt, and bridges so wrapt in their dreams they fall into the river.

What intrigued Ludvik most were the embedded images, the fragments of pictures included in other pictures, this play of distorting mirrors, these fine lacerations in the surface of the visible world, in whose chinks other plastic forms come welling up. Images winking with unmistakable irony, or melancholy, serious or playful, erotic or pensive, depending on Kolar's mood, and what the viewer's eye sees. And then there were the portraits: in some of them, Ludvik sometimes thought he could see something of the enigma of the face emerging. Crushed, deformed, or geometrically dismantled countenances, letting glimpses of other faces, bodies, settings and places, other architectures issue from the cracks between the fragments. Hinterlands lying behind foreheads, eyelids, in the hollow of cheeks, and mouths.

In one portrait Ludvik caught a glimpse of himself – just as fragmented as the face of the model. A cut-up Baudelaire on a reflective background, suddenly confronting the passer-by with his shattered image enmeshed with the viewer's own face, like a visual echo of his challenge to every reader of the *Flowers of Evil*: 'hypocrite reader, my fellow, my brother!' But far from being drawn into tortuous Baudelairean torments, Ludvik merely felt somewhat dispossessed of himself – he perceived himself as absent. He turned away with a vague feeling of unease, and continued his visit, applying himself to jotting down a few notes for an article he was intending to write.

When he emerged from the House of the Stone Bell, the light was already fading. For a moment Ludvik's perception and thoughts carried on operating in the same way as Kolar, by means of fragmentation, confrontation, collage and intersection. The result was a hybrid vision: a cut-out of his own face enshrining Esther's, all in shades of autumn leaves. He dismissed the image and hurried towards the metro. But he must have lingered a little too long in the world according to Kolar and his mind had acquired a few creases, strange shifts of thought and vision – Kolar creases. In the entrance of the station where he got off, a young man was distributing advertising leaflets. Ludvik automatically took one and, when he cast a distracted eye over the sheet before throwing it in a dustbin, superimposed on the publicity blurb he read an old poem of Kolar's which he was unaware of having memorized:

Search through your memory
through history
search through literature
for a couple of lovers
who died
without having celebrated their wedding

Get their names printed
on wedding invitations
and distribute them to passers-by in the street
on the very same day
at the very same time
given on the invitations for the ceremony.

As soon as it had passed through his mind, the poem gave way to another thought. 'It's All Saints' Day soon,' it suddenly occurred to Ludvik, and he imperceptibly shrugged his shoulders. But irritated by these unexpected memories that his visit to the House of the Stone Bell had stirred, he put off till later writing the article he wanted to devote to the Kolar exhibition.

And then it was All Saints' Day: announcements of past weddings flourished in profusion on tombstones sheltering husbands, wives, lovers, mistresses, who died decades ago, or just a few years; announcements of grief and mourning burned in pink tremulous rush-lights beneath oval portraits of the deceased whose smiles grew ever fainter. Then the November rains washed away both flowers and flames. All that remained were mossy-winged angels standing among the tombs like announcements of eternity, and the stray cats that prowled the paths.

Ludvik's prowling was confined to inside his head. He wandered slowly in search of ideas and enthusiasm, for he was supposed to be doing a translation that did not greatly inspire him, and he had an article to write.

One morning he went into his local bank. He went

up to the counter for cash withdrawals. There was an employee he had never seen before behind the glass screen. He had a smooth round head and thick silver-rimmed spectacles. Ludvik handed him the form on which he had written down his savings' account password, and the teller, quickly picking up the piece of paper and barely glancing at it, croaked this password under his breath.

'The Joker, ah hah!'

To Ludvik, the man bore an unfortunate resemblance to a frog. The said frog tapped at his computer to check the state of the account and launched into a convoluted tirade.

'The Joker! Humph! A fine name for a passbook! If you think you'll make your savings grow with a name like that! Perhaps you thought this Tarot character, because he has a name and not a number, was open to infinite interpretation? Well, no, this numberless arcanum is equivalent to zero and isn't even counted in the total of a pack of cards. The Joker is just a tramp, a wandering beggar disguised as a fool, wearing bells round his neck like lunatics and lepers, and torn breeches. And the bundle he carries around on his shoulder, have you seen that? It's flat, as empty as this foolish fellow's head. The Joker is someone who's incapable of acquiring anything, and what's more he loses everything . . .'

'I'm not interested in the Tarot,' Ludvik threw in, to interrupt this crank, but the fellow continued his harangue, regardless.

'It remains to be seen whether what the Joker loses is good or bad. Is it his time and energy that he squanders, in fruitless wanderings? For, have you considered, sir, the value of time? Oh, I'm not asking you this question as a banker, far from it! Time is the small change we're allocated in order to pay for our admittance to eternity later on. Woe betide us if we wantonly waste it. We blow away our lives like dandelion clocks, and soon the heart is denuded. In the Apocalypse are written these dreadful words: 'Behold, I come as a thief. Blessed is he that watcheth, and keepeth his garments, Lest he walk naked, and they see his shame.'

'I don't care any more about the Apocalypse than I do about the Tarot,' cried Ludvik, 'I'm only here to take out some money, not to be subjected to a sermon!'

'A little patience,' said the frog, without taking his eyes off his keyboard, and he continued his preaching with renewed fervour. 'All right, the Joker's an inauspicious will-o'-the-wisp, but his folly is double-edged. And it's the same with salt, which can be either caustic or purificatory. Have you noticed, sir, what the tip of this vagabond's yellow hat is embellished with? It's not a pompon, nor a bell, but a little red disk. Setting sun, autumn sun, red moon or fiery planet? This lurid little star behind the Joker's head is the last spark of reason remaining to him, the last ember of conscience. That's all it takes to get a big fire going again. So he hasn't lost everything. Having reduced his past and all his belongings to nothing, he has thereby laid himself open to the unexpected, the unhoped-for. To eternity. Yes, maybe it's a good thing to go round like that, with your head in the clouds, with empty pockets and a heart riddled with poverty, and a yen for boundlessness. To wander, on and on, always off the beaten track, forging your way over rocks and scrubland . . .'

'And I've got to be on my way, I'm in a hurry,' said Ludvik, banging the glass with his fist.

'I've nearly finished,' said the other, tapping away at his computer with increasing feverishness. He gave the impression of striking the keys at random. And he went on doggedly: 'The Joker comes along unexpectedly, and the love of wide open spaces in his eyes dethrones queens and checkmates kings. He is the insolent fool who trims with wind the ermine cloak of the powerful, who blanches the royal purple, and exposes his buttocks to the crown. He is the coefficient of expansion that denounces the vanity of possessions and the glories of this world, the allurement of all power, by causing them to swell up like empty waterskins. In this case, the Joker is a sage, a mystic. Did you intend it in that sense, sir, when you chose the name of the Joker as a password for your savings' book?'

And once again without bothering to wait for an answer from Ludvik, he brought his ten fingers down on the keyboard as if he were striking a chord, then swivelled round on his chair, turned to a till from which he extracted a few banknotes, and finally came up to the window. He pressed his batrachian face to the glass. His hair was the colour of rancid butter, smoothed back.

'Here's your money,' he said, unceremoniously passing the notes over the counter.

Ludvik noticed that he had long tapering fingernails, much too long for his little podgy fingers. He felt like shouting at him, but restrained himself for fear of unleashing another avalanche of nonsense. He contented himself with picking up the banknotes and counting them. While he was checking them, the fellow suddenly spun round in his chair on wheels, and using his feet on the ground to propel himself, went speeding out of his aquarium, shouting, 'May a fair wind blow on the wasteland!'

Ludvik looked up just in time to see the back of the chair and a big round head with a scrawny pony-tail over the top of it. 'A tadpole's tail!' thought Ludvik with disgust.

By the time he got home, he had already forgotten the incident. Only the cry of 'May a fair wind blow on the wasteland' intermittently came into his mind. These gusts of wind, however ridiculous they might have been, proved envigorating, for Ludvik settled down to work again with an energy he had not had for a long time. He polished off a chapter of the book he had to translate, then scribbled a few lines on the subject of Kolar, on his art of atomizing the manifest aspects of the visible world, of cutting breaches of strangeness in the most famous and familiar of paintings, of restoring to us what we thought we knew, seen in a strange way, of making us see again what lies dormant deep in the pupils of our eyes.

He was still ferreting in the labyrinths laid out by Kolar in the underside of the visible world, when the telephone rang. It was Eva calling to tell him that her uncle had suffered another stroke the previous week.

'He's very much weaker,' she said, 'he no longer has the strength or the desire to eat, and his breathing has become laboured.' Not really knowing what to say, Ludvik offered to come to T, but there was no sense in it.

'It's very kind of you,' said Eva, 'but I'm afraid the days for visiting are over, Joachym doesn't really seem to see people, at least not the way the rest of us do. He looks straight through everything, as if everything were transparent.'

'Transparent?'

'Yes,' Eva continued, 'his eyes stray aimlessly even when you bend your face right over him to speak to him, and he makes vague gestures in the air in slow motion, as if he were trying to catch something, or to follow the lines of a half-obliterated text.'

At the word 'text', Ludvik jumped. He recalled the train incident, and dreading that Eva might ask him a question about the notebook, he cut short the conversation. He hung up, his conscience troubled, and his heart a little heavy. Then he remembered the way Brum used always to accompany his words with slow gestures, following the cadence of his phrases, to emphasize certain words. And when he read a text, particularly when he recited a poem that suddenly slipped into his mind, he would mark the rhythm of the lines with his slender fingers. One day, during a lesson in which he had dwelt on Novalis's *Hymns to the Night*, Brum had then moved on to Rilke's *Poems to the*

Night. From one song of darkness to another. And as he was intoning one verse in his deep voice in which the underlying texture of his breathing was audible, Ludvik thought for a moment that he could see certain words glowing on Brum's fingertips, that he could feel the sounds quivering in the moted shaft of light from the window.

'Dreaming is brocade that trails behind you,
dreaming is a tree, a fleeting brilliance,
a sound –;
a feeling that begins and ends in you
is dreaming; an animal that looks you in the eye
is dreaming; an angel who takes pleasure in you
is dreaming. Dreaming is the word that with a
gentle fall
falls into your consciousness like a petal
that catches in your hair; luminous, enlaced and
subdued –,
if you raise your hands: still, dreaming comes
it comes falling into them like a ball –
nearly everything dreams but you carry it all.

That day everything was devoted to the act of dreaming, even the specks of dust in the rays of light, and above all, Brum's entire being, flesh and breath. And the mystery of dreaming, so tenderly, so disturbingly entwined with the substance of things, with the flow of air, with the texture of the hour, settled everywhere in glimmerings and quiverings.

Brum had to such an extent carried 'all' within him – this murmur of the world, this stirring of time, the bright eddies of daylight and the slow eddyings of the dark – he had given such verve, such tone to silence, that, now he was unable to help himself any more, 'all' had to help him. Had to carry him along like a raft made of straw to the deep, infinitely clear waters of the invisible. So Ludvik would have liked to believe.

The first snow fell, but did not last long. However, what did take hold was the cold. The trees were totally bare, the pedestrians completely muffled up, the former very still and charcoal grey, the latter very hurried and red-faced, and once again Ludvik accredited to the former the advantage of dignity. But one day when he was considering this, an untimely image sprang into his mind, and blocked his thought; an extremely absurd image, however, that of the frog in the bank who had concluded his rant by bringing his ten fingers down simultaneously on his computer keyboard.

That same day, while he was waiting for a tram, sheltering from the rain under a big black umbrella with a wooden handle in the shape of a duck's head, a young man came running up, and drawing very close to him, asked if he could take refuge under his umbrella until his tram arrived.

'It's not that I'm afraid of the rain,' said the intruder, who was all streaming wet, 'but it's to protect my flower, it's so fragile, it's likely to dissolve . . .'

Ludvik raised his eyebrows, then the young man opened his dubious beige parka and revealed a glimpse of the soluble flower he was holding very carefully under the lining. A strange flower, with bizarre petals, like tumescent growths, with semi-transparent grey surfaces and a glassy stem spiked with thorns and irregular-shaped leaves.

'It's a salt rose,' said the young man with a big smile, 'it took me weeks to grow it. Isn't it beautiful?'

'Uh, yes, yes . . .' Ludvik agreed, scratching his ear a little.

The young man extracted the saline rose from his bosom and slowly turned round in front of Ludvik's eyes.

'The structure's made of wire that I then wrapped round with string, after which I immersed the whole thing in a bowlful of salt-saturated water, but in several stages: first the corolla, then the stem. It's beautiful, isn't it?'

'Absolutely, absolutely . . .'

But the stranger did not seem concerned about Ludvik's opinion, the repetition of his question more of a kind of exclamation. While contemplating his rose, which he kept twirling under Ludvik's nose, he went on, 'Having been created by the evaporation of water, it would die if it was rained on too heavily. Flowers don't like violence. My rose was born very slowly, it blossomed out of patience.'

'But if you're so worried about your flower,' said Ludvik, 'why did you come out in this pouring rain with it?'

'Oh, that's a secret, between the rose and me! When the time comes, you have to hurry.'

'Yes, of course,' said Ludvik, increasingly convinced that he was dealing with a harmless eccentric, but as there were times when he was not averse to this very heterogeneous category of people, he continued the conversation under the umbrella with raindrops violently drumming on it.

'So, just like that, all of a sudden, it was a matter of urgency?'

'The young man did not reply straightaway. He tilted his head slightly to one side, with a weary, rather sad look, and for a moment tapped his lips with the fingertips of his free hand. His nails were chewed and the skin around them all raw.

'No, not just like that, not all of sudden,' he said finally. 'The urgency dates back a long way. But it becomes evident unexpectedly. Roses, which feed on patience as much as light, have a very fine, very acute sense of these tiny mysteries of time that pass unnoticed, or as the vagaries of chance, to the eyes of unobservant people, but chance is by no means as whimsical and inconsequential as people generally like to believe. A salt rose knows this just as well, if not better than, a natural rose.'

'But what exactly does it know?'

Then the young man's expression and tone of voice suddenly changed, hardened, became almost annoyed.

'What does it know? But it's up to you to find out! After all, you have a shared memory in the distant origins of time, in the depths of primordial seas. Retrace your thoughts beyond the narrow circle of your preconceived, indeed ill-conceived, overrated ideas, venture into the unthought-of . . . ah, but here's my tram!'

And he left Ludvik standing there, as he disappeared into the first car with his rose held close to his chest again, under his parka. Ludvik took the precaution of getting into the rear car, for while he enjoyed the imaginative fancy of harmless eccentrics he did not on the other hand relish bombastic crackpots. This reminded him of the incident in the bank, and he wondered if a epidemic of looniness was spreading through town. He could certainly see several points of resemblance between the esoteric frog of the earlier incident and this excitable young fellow with the salt rose, but he did not linger on these similarities. Suddenly his thoughts strayed towards memories that he did not in fact like to recall. Esther, again. Roses were her favourite flowers. There was a time when she used to dry the most beautiful of the ones that Ludvik gave her, and with these she would create new bouquets, in faded colours, with thin breakable stems, extremely fragile petals. Some of these petals sometimes became detached and fell off like wing sheaths of dull yellow, or purplish red, like dead fingernails, like eyelids weary of brooding on a thought dwelt on for too long. And Esther too grew weary one day; she threw away her bouquets of dead roses, pretty relics of their love whose dreams she had reduced to dust, whose fragrance she had allowed to grow musty, and whose memory she had repudiated. Ludvik shook his head to clear it of this recollection, to shake himself free of a bad dream.

*

Snow fell again, more heavily and more lasting this time. The town was getting ready to celebrate Christmas in great winter style.

And Brum? Ludvik suddenly wondered with concern, one morning as he went out into the street, as if the reverberation of the light on the snow-covered branches of the trees had just illuminated a corner of his brain that he had overlooked. He hesitated, then finally decided to call Eva. She told him that her uncle was slowly fading, and that according to the doctors there was no hope for him any more. They were even amazed that Brum was still alive, capable sometimes of surprising bursts of energy which made him sit up in bed, and utter a few words in a distinct voice; they could not understand where the dying old man managed to find the strength to keep going the way he did. Then she added a few words that once again sounded very mystifying to Ludvik: 'My uncle is not done yet with surprising the doctors, for the hour of his deliverance is not as close at hand as they believe. He'll hold out until the day comes.'

Ludvik asked her what day she was referring to, but she gave an even more sibylline response.

'A day far back in history.'

He dared not insist for fear that she might start talking about the notebook in which Brum may have mentioned something about this. So he remained perplexed.

Christmas cards began to arrive in Ludvik's letterbox. Among these cards he found one neither whose image nor message scribbled on the back he could understand. To tell the truth, the image was non-existent, or practically; a swirl of creamy white, reminiscent of a puddle of curdled milk, a little creased and yellowed in places. The text was also obscure: a few lines in sepia-coloured ink in ill-formed scratchy handwriting that Ludvik could not decipher. He did not waste much time trying to decode this scrawl, the formulas for Christmas wishes being all more or less the same. As for the signature, it was completely illegible – a kind of seismographic line. He reflected for a moment, waving the card like a fan, trying to work out which of his acquaintances could possibly wield a pen with such ineptitude, but could not think of anyone. He finally gave up and, putting the card on a shelf, soon forgot about it.

His translation progressed ever more slowly. The author of the work often referred to Rabbi Loew, the Maharal of Prague, about whom Ludvik knew only the legends that had grown up round his mysterious personality, but nothing about the thinking and the work that lay, vast and obscure, behind the eccentric image of fable. He began to note down the passages that were giving him problems so that he could go and do some research in the library. This reminded him of his youth, when he used to spend whole days studying in the reading room of the Klementinum.

Christmas went by without his noticing. The evening of the Nativity, he lingered in a café playing billiards, the only game he liked to play. A game wonderfully suited to his taste for silence and solitude. When he came out after a long session playing by himself, the streets were empty, the windows of the houses brightly lit up. As he emerged into a square he saw a large number of people coming down the steps of the church that stood in the centre. From the open door poured a straw-coloured light that seemed to be gently shepherding all the faithful towards the porch. Off they went, tottering, or dancing, along the slippery paths across the square, whose grass plots glittered with mica-like snow. Ludvik thought of Brum. In what dream was he drifting as he lay on his hospital bed under the intrigued eyes of the doctors? Was he returning to childhood? But then, what distress, what destitution of childhood run wild must he have to endure! An inverse Nativity, moved to a different place, no longer in Bethlehem, but at Gethsemane.

He went home. Before going to bed, he glanced through the notes he had made in his notebook, then sat down for a moment in front of his computer to look through the two chapters he had already translated, but with certain passages left blank. Rabbi Loew accounted for the gaps in the text which turned out to be more difficult than Ludvik had at first thought. As he stood up, he caught sight of the pale card he had put on the shelf. Seen under the electric light, and not by daylight, it appeared slightly different: the white of the image was more full of nuances than appeared at first sight. Vague shapes were discernible on the left-hand side of the image, but painted almost tint on tint, with a barely detectable variation of shade between ivory white and eggshell white. He hesitated to throw this card away, then finally put it back in the same place.

He spent New Year's Eve with some friends. One of them told quite a funny story, brought back from his parents' village in Slovakia, where he had been to spend Christmas.

For years, angry villagers had found themselves powerless faced with the disappearance of all the ribbons decorating the wreathes and bouquets laid on tombs when burials took place. The very next day after the funeral not a single funerary ribbon remained. But the thief did not seem totally ungodly, for no flowers were stolen. Whether fresh flowers or plastic, they were left neatly laid out on the grave. The beautiful ribbons embellished with eternal regrets were all that was taken. But these pilferings were resented as so many outrages and desecrations by the shawl-clad vestal virgins of the old cemetery who railed against the thief, calling it a scandal, and even blaming the devil. For no one had any idea who it could possibly be that kept on perpetrating this injury to the dead and their grieving families. Was it some criminal of flesh and bone or some malefic spirit. And with what perverse intention or even dark design, was he stealing these adornments of mortuary flowers? A watch was mounted, traps were laid, to no avail. As a matter of prudence, the zealous old women one day asked the priest to come and recite prayers of exorcism within the walls of the cemetery, in case they were dealing with a marauding demon, or the perverse soul of a sinner who had died unshriven and was thus taking revenge for his posthumous torments by snitching the pious tokens left on the graves of the honest dead. But it was no good, the thefts continued.

This last Christmas finally brought a resolution. After morning service, when all the flock were returning home, big fat Ludmilla, one of the village crones, slipped on the icy road. Down she went, with her skirts flying up round her chin. Then the answer to the mystery was revealed to her companions scurrying by. Ludmilla's petticoats were decorated all over with the famous ribbons that had disappeared. She had sewn them so artfully on to her undergarments that it would never have occurred to anyone to look for them there. So for years, unbeknown to anyone, Ludmilla had been going around with her buttocks kept warm under petticoats that were trimmed with eternal regrets and lyrical expressions of sorrow. And this filled her with a melancholy joy. It was her sweet mournful secret. In the rustle of her petticoats, she, and she alone, could detect the sighs of desolation, the trickle of tears, mumurs from beyond the grave. But because of her fateful tumble, her very private communings with the dead were now at an end; the other old ladies, in a fit of holy anger, stripped her of blasphemous petticoats. And now poor Ludmilla's buttocks must be in mourning and her heart left in the cold.

The account of this burlesque drama cheered up Ludvik, as if Ludmilla's petticoats had wiped away the anxious thoughts and obscure doubts that for some time had been intruding on his mind more and more. After all, all these pseudo-mysteries unfolding around him, as if nothing were going on, were perhaps as harmless and absurd as that which had so long surrounded the disappearance of the funerary ribbons.

And the count went up, with another figure added to the century's total. The Christmas card that remained anonymous continued to display its whiteness on the shelf. Ludvik, who spent long hours in front of his computer tinkering with his translation, liked to rest his gaze on the creamy-white rectangle whenever he looked up from the screen that tired his eyes. It calmed him, it was a kind of little window that opened on to a cloudy emptiness in which a swirl of shapes sometimes took form, but so faintly, so intangibly, that he was never quite sure of what he thought he could glimpse.

One morning he went to the library to consult some reference books, looking for information about Rabbi Loew. His notebook was beginning to look like a spider's web with laboriously woven threads that were still far from being connected.

When he emerged from the Klementinum's courtyard, at about one o'clock, the sky suddenly cleared and the sun, as white as cuttlebone, shone brightly, very high overhead. This sudden flood of light made the sky turn blue and the snow on the roofs glisten. Rabbi Loew's statue, standing at the corner of the town hall, glittered with frost, and the snow, gathered in drifts on the slender young girl standing naked at his side, like a staff seeking support, gathered on her cheek, her hair and in the base of the curve of her spine, running down her back, hips and thighs as it melted. She looked like an exhausted swimmer who gives up battling against the seas, slowly sinking, vertically, into the depths. An undine covered with foam, returning to the darkness and the silence of deep waters. The Maharal's long wavy beard looked like silvery seaweed, and he like a guardian spirit of Arctic waters.

Ludvik, who usually paid no attention to this statue when he passed by, so much part of the urban landscape was it, studied it more closely. The fact was that Great Rabbi Loew had been giving him difficulty for some time. He had been reading the rabbi's most important work, *The Well of Exile*, and, with Ladislav Saloun's sculpture in front of him, he recalled the opening verses of the chapter on 'The Fifth Well', which he had just been reading:

> In the fifth well, there are deep waters;
> Embedded in their depths are precious stones;
> those who can swim collect pearls,
> they look like the smooth pebbles in a mountain stream and
> are reminiscent of distant fields and stones;
> But these stones are lightning bright
> casting their brilliance to the ends of the world.

The Maharal and the young nymph clutching his arm came from just such deep, ice-cold waters; he a rock caught in the torrent, she an aquatic plant entwined round the rock.

A big, rugged, furrowed boulder, he glittered from

the depths of centuries past from which he had drawn his knowledge and forged his wisdom, she glistened from the depths of time immemorial from which she had drawn her slumber and forged her madness.

But the sky clouded over again, and the sculpture took on a leaden hue as it fell into shadow; it seemed to huddle in the niche in the wall and there was no longer anything aquatic about the Maharal's tall draped body. Matter alone asserted itself, massive and dark, as if it needed remodelling. And it was exactly like this, hard and obscure, that his texts would continue to impose themselves on Ludvik.

He set off for a walk round the neighbourhood, and went into a bar. The room was smoky, noisy. He ordered a beer at the counter. While the barman was rinsing a tankard before filling it up for him, a customer standing at the bar slowly raised his glassful of slivovic in Ludvik's direction. He was a man of about fifty, dressed with an elegance somewhat out of keeping with these surroundings. He even wore fine leather gloves and a wide-brimmed felt hat, all in mouse grey, like his coat and his scarf.

'To Caspar!' he said, as he raised his glass and drained it in one.

Ludvik did not understand to the health of which Caspar he was thus knocking back his glass of spirits, so he contented himself with replying to this uncertain toast with a curt nod. The elegantly dressed man clicked his tongue, then clinked his glass on the counter, indicating to the barman to serve him another drink. The barman, who had a moustache as droopy as his eyelids and his paunch, pushed a tankard overflowing with foam towards Ludvik and poured another slivovic for the mouse-grey man. The man performed the same gesture as before, but this time with the words, 'To Melchior!' And again he drained his glass, then silently asked for a third refill.

'It's a good thing there are only three mages,' thought Ludvik, who finally understood what this was all about, 'unless he's also going to drink a toast to the shepherds!'

And the stranger went through the same routine. 'To Balthasar!' And he swigged his last glass, which he then set upside down on the counter. His royal progress was over.

'That's what you call celebrating the Epiphany!' said the barman with a lopsided smile, which momentarily upset the symmetry of his walrus moustache, then he plunged his hands back into the sink, almost up to the elbows, and lost interest in the king drinker.

The stranger moved a bit closer to Ludvik and started up a conversation.

'I've always liked the legend of the three wise men, but for a long time there was something about them that bothered me. Why, when they came to prostrate themselves before the divine newborn child, did they only offer him gold, frankincense and myrrh?'

'They weren't familiar with slivovic,' replied Ludvik, sipping his beer.

'That's not the reason, and you know it. Think about it, they offer him gold, mineral light, the concretion of solar tears, and aromatic resins that only release their power under the slow effect of heat. Yet there's another substance connected with heat, abounding in flavour and purificatory virtues.'

'Hm,' said Ludvik, who suddenly felt on the defensive, but the stranger went on:

'Salt! Fire yielded by water, grains of pure light extracted from the bowels of the earth. But this treasure was not one of the gifts of the three kings. Why not? This preoccupied me for some time. And yet the answer's so simple! Why indeed would they have given salt to a child, when that very child was bringing to the world the most intense taste of salt?'

The unease that Ludvik had felt beginning to stir inside him a moment ago soon increased. Was it no longer possible to step outside or go into a bar without being besieged by some nuisance holding forth about salt? He set his still half-full tankard down on the counter and turned on his heels, ignoring the man in grey, who directed a few more words at his back.

'No, I won't suppress the still small voice of this star over the desert, amid the silence of the sands and the night, in the shadow of . . .' But his voice was lost in the hubbub of the smoky room. Outside it was drizzling a little melted snow.

Ludvik went home. Having no desire to settle down to work again, after wandering round aimlessly and nibbling a few slices of salami, he was suddenly taken with a fancy to soak in a hot bath. As he splashed his toes in the bath foam, which gave off a strong smell of pine, he reflected on the killjoy at the bar who had spoilt the pleasure of drinking his beer. At this point he also reflected on the story of the three wise men. Of the Epiphany, as indeed of all the other liturgical feasts, he retained only a distant memory, reduced to a few trite images. The three kings from the Orient, wearing exotic headdresses, sumptuous cloaks and gemstones, and each one bearing a gleaming coffer; a string of camels accompanying the procession, outlined against an extremely starry night, and an Infant Jesus sitting enthroned in the hay, a pink baby sovereign. It had never before occurred to Ludvik to challenge this faded cliché or, more to the point, to take any interest in it at all. And now suddenly for the first time this image appeared to him in a new light: the cliché shook itself out, like a stuffed animal suddenly coming to life again and throwing off both the dust and the gilding with which it was covered, and the three mages started to stir in Ludvik's imagination. In slow motion. Ludvik saw them walking, barefoot and bareheaded. Dressed in long grey robes, they went without vainglory, with no entourage, their thin hands cupped round clay bowls. But Ludvik did not know what these bowls contained, perhaps they were empty. The three figures progressed for a while against the background of darkness. As for the Infant, Ludvik could not see him, and could not tell whether he lay ahead or behind on the route the Magi were following, or indeed whether the latter were returning or arriving.

When he got out of the bath, it was almost dark. Already in advance, he felt it was a very long evening. He flicked through his address book and called a girlfriend with whom he was having an intermittent relationship. An hour later he was at her place, and the next hour in her bed, where they spent the evening. But as soon as he had satisfied his sexual desire, Ludvik felt himself at a complete loss. He got up, with the excuse of going to drink a glass of water. He lingered for a long time in the kitchen, where, for want of anything better to do, he lit a whole big boxful of matches, one by one, then peeled the skin off an orange in a complete spiral. He returned to the bedroom with the orange wrapped up in its peel again. Katia had fallen asleep, lying on her stomach across the bed, with her arms in an arc above her head. He lifted the bedspread and gazed for a moment at Katia's naked body. He knew its texture, smell, curves and softness, but not its internal landscapes, and the quiet murmur of its blood, its breath, its dreams – and he did not want to know them. Katia remained a stranger to him, although a familiar one. She shivered; he covered her up again. Then he took the orange out of its peel, separated each segment which he lay in a halo round the sleeping girl's dishevelled hair, and finally wrapped the spiral of peel round her left wrist. After which, he quietly left.

The vision of the three Magi that Ludvik had in his bath came back to him every now and again, and it was always the same black and grey image, the same slow motion. The three distant figures were outlined against the darkness, creeping forward with tiny, sometimes stumbling, footsteps. Where were they going, wondered Ludvik. What were they looking for? Who were they looking for?

And what if it were Brum these ash-grey Magi were making their way towards in this way, Ludvik said to himself one day. He called Eva. In her usual rather distant tone of voice, she told him that her uncle's condition continued to deteriorate, bedsores were beginning to consume his body that had for too long been bedridden, and the doctors' amazement grew in proportion to the physical decline of this dying man who nevertheless would not let go his hold on life. She spoke too of his ever more transparent gaze, which seemed to pursue some distant objective, somewhere in the invisible world. And again she played the Sphinx, which exasperated Ludvik, who had become allergic to anyone who talked in riddles.

'When he's reached that objective, he'll lay down his arms.'

He did not allow himself to make any comment, feeling ever more bound to caution because of the loss of Brum's notebook.

One very frosty morning, as he was crossing the square in the Old Town on his way to the Klementinum where he was continuing his research, Ludvik saw a policeman go jogging by. With as much grace as if brandishing a truncheon, he was clutching a red rose, all tied up in its white-spotted cellophane wrapper. He was just as red as his flower and a little cloud of vapour floated in front of his mouth. To which sweetheart was this chilled lover hurrying to carry his flower? No, the impression he gave was more that of running towards a police station to deliver a conclusive piece of criminal evidence he had just discovered. What if, nearly four centuries on, this were the famous flower whose fragrance killed the Great Rabbi Loew, the man whom death could not catch except by cunning, burying itself in the heart of a rose offered to the rabbi in all innocence by his beloved granddaughter?

Ludvik had no sooner formulated this conjecture than the policeman slipped and went sprawling at the foot of the Jan Hus's pyre. But he fell handsomely, kept his hand raised, so that the rose he was holding stood upright beneath the martyr's hand, as though waiting for his benediction. Finally he got to his feet, looked round furiously, and set off again more cautiously. He was limping a little, but the flower was intact, as a piece of evidence should be, whether criminal evidence or a testimony of love.

Ludvik worked at the library until late. From his extensive checking of archives and documents, he had gathered all the information he needed to complete his translation. His notebook was full of jottings, dates, names and concepts, Hebrew, Greek and Latin terms, quotations; the spider's web had proliferated, its threads branching out, knitting together, bifurcating, creating new nodes. Ludvik had in fact dug up and accumulated much more than was needed, but he had got involved in the game – a game of following paths of investigation, which had led him into what was going on behind the scenes in the 16th century; into the cabinets of artistic wonders and curiosities of nature for which princes and kings of the time had a craze; into the labyrinths of anamorphic paintings, those visual puzzles that revealed the reverse side of the constructed world and of history; and also into the corridors of Hradsin Castle at the time of Emperor Rudolf II, and into the lanes of the ghetto huddled in the shadow of the castle, where the Great Rabbi Loew worked and died at the end of a long life that was dedicated to meditation for nearly a century.

While Ludvik may have been unenthusiastic at first about translating this book which a publishing house had commissioned from him, and which he had agreed to do for want of any other work, he was now beginning to take an interest and even a certain pleasure in this translation job that was prompting him to explore a century in which he detected many things in common with his own century. People, then, had wrestled with intellectual doubts, amazements and fears that caused Ludvik's contemporaries to stumble even more tragically. The latter might well take up, with greater voice, the poet John Donne's lament, faced with the collapse of the old cosmic order:

> ' 'Tis all in pieces, all coherence gone,
> All just supply and all Relation.'

It had already been the case for a long time that any meaning to be found in the world only allowed itself to be apprehended by indirect routes, by the suspension and even the overthrow of thought.

But Ludvik now had to sort out and classify all

these notes that he had been so overzealous in gathering, and had jotted down chaotically in his notebook. So he stopped going to the library for a while and continued his work at home. He was soon feeling cross with himself for having accumulated so many references, and especially for his lack of rigour and method; dates were crowded on the page, in no chronological order, and furthermore switched between two calendars, the Hebrew and the Christian. He had sometimes forgotten to keep a record of the source of the quotations he had dug up, or else he had copied down some fragments of text too hurriedly and could not always read his own handwriting. While he had enjoyed browsing through the memory of a century full of upheaval, of discoveries and inventions, he now regretted his carelessness as a poor scribe. And this deciphering of his own handwriting, alternating with long hours spent in front of his computer screen, on which he would scroll the text of his translation so as to fill in the gaps that still dotted it, put increasing strain on his eyes. He kept pressing his fingers against his eyelids, beneath which bright rings would then dance feverishly, or from time to time he would allow his gaze to stray to the pale card that had the virtue of relieving his eyes. Occasionally he thought he could see a vague image emerge from this tone-on-tone painting – outlines of figures subtlely worked in ivory following each other in single file through a milky fog. This formed a pendant to the haunting grey-and-black image of the Magi that had been returning to his thoughts fairly regularly over the past month or so, and was always associated in his mind with the slow, very slow death of Brum, who continued to defy the doctors' prognostications ever more brazenly. Grey kings against a background of night, ivory kings against a background of pale dawn, all wending their way on the verge of the invisible and the motionless, and all looking like beggar kings. A single image and its negative, but impossible to say which took precedence over the other.

Ludvik assessed the amount of work he had left to do to finish his translation and considered it wiser to call on his publisher and try to persuade him to allow him more time. The publisher proved very understanding, even a little too understanding, as he gave his translator almost unlimited respite, for the disastrous reason that his company was going bankrupt because the costs of production and distribution were so high, while sales were always falling. Anyway, the insolvent publisher added, with a mixture of bitterness and resignation and a third glassful of Georgian brandy, it certainly was not with a work like the one Ludvik was translating that sales were going to pick up again. Nevertheless, he was very keen on this book, and he encouraged Ludvik to complete his translation, for if he was going to go under, he said, it might as well be in style, with head held high and a stout heart. Ludvik asked him why he was interested in this text, and the publisher replied with an evasive gesture, 'Rabbi Loew is one of those people who have the gift of telling us something new about ourselves and about the world irrespective of the age. Things that we need to know, more than ever. All the same, we have to feel this need. Otherwise what he tells us will remain a dead letter.'

Ludvik got news about himself and about the world two days later, but though they were not quite so fresh as they might have been, they were no less topical. It was not the Great Rabbi Loew who brought this news. Ludvik had decided to take a break from his translation, since his publisher was being as generous with time as he was short of money. The out-of-date messenger was a very modest individual: an old newspaper vendor, freezing in his kiosk, near the top of Korunni Street.

'The evening paper, please,' Ludvik said, searching his pockets for some change.

'Evening or morning, midday or midnight, yesterday's or today's, what difference does it make?' muttered the newspaper vendor, of whom only his head and shoulders were visible behind the counter. He was wearing a dark-grey corduroy cap that partly concealed his hair and his forehead; very deep lines radiated from his eyes to his temples and furrowed his hollow cheeks. His greying moustache was stained brown with tobacco.

'It's like the weather forecasts,' replied Ludvik, 'they change from hour to hour, you might just as well keep up to date with whatever the current temperature is wherever you happen to be.'

'Yeah,' said the man, not moving, 'rain one minute, fine weather the next, a cold snap, then milder temperatures, a period of drought, then frost;

there's a limit to the number of ways the dice can fall, it's always the same sets of figures that keep turning up. You pick them up and roll them again; it's the same with events, first war, then peace. But there's far more bad weather than good, and the violent and the wicked outnumber the few just men.'

'That's for sure,' admitted Ludvik, 'all the same, though, it's better to know more or less what's happening, sometimes it makes it possible to limit the damage.'

'Oh, yes, is that what you think? When the more they overwhelm us with information, often contradictory and sometimes downright mendacious, and spiced up with piquant images, into the bargain, or even stuffed with adulterated ingredients, the less we know about it. Because knowing doesn't mean ingurgitating kilos of images and verbiage; we're crammed full, and suffering from indigestion, but since we're intoxicated, we ask for more. No, knowing isn't seeing everything and hearing everything in bulk, it's learning first of all to select, to consider carefully, to look and listen from the depths of your heart and your mind, and not from the tips of your nerves or your emotions.'

As he spoke, he rolled two cigarettes and offered one to Ludvik. Prominent veins gave his hands a purplish hue, and his fingernails were flecked with white. Ludvik accepted the cigarette somewhat reluctantly. The vendor lit it for him, holding his lighter through the kiosk hatch, then he resumed his train of thought.

'Limit the damage, you were saying? There was a

time when you could believe that: when the gates of the concentration camps were opened, and the full horror of what had been done finally came to light, people said that if they'd known in time what was going on, they wouldn't have allowed it to happen, and the world swore never to let barbarism triumph again in that way. Well, barbarism's thriving, it's been taken as an example and acquired a large following, and as it increases, so do the number of charnel houses, without the rest of the world – including us, sir – falling to its knees with tears of blood, shame, and sorrow, or taking up arms against the assassins. As you very well know, there are numerous cases of atrocities all over the planet. You read the papers, so you know about them. Tell me, then, how do you limit the damage?'

Ludvik thought, 'I'll take take one last drag of this damned cigarette and then I'm out of here.'

But, as if he had been reading his thoughts, the vendor said, 'It's not very good tobacco, I agree, it's quite bitter, and what I've got to say is not much better. Yet despite my age, I still can't get used to the excesses of human madness: all this hatred, this fury lurking in the hearts of so many people, or this great cowardice ensconced in the hearts of so many others . . . But here, have a little coffee, it'll warm you up.'

And he produced a thermos flask that he kept under his chair, unscrewed the lid and poured some coffee into two plastic cups. 'It's already sugared,' he said, 'and laced with a drop of rum. You need some help to withstand this cold.'

And Ludvik felt obliged to accept, in spite of his desire to get away. The cup scalded his fingers, while his feet were numb with cold. The vendor, of course, took the opportunity to prolong the conversation.

'Fifteen years ago, I visited Auschwitz-Birkenau concentration camp. I thought I already knew about it all, I'd seen and read a great deal on the subject. But when I found myself physically on that silent and deserted site, everything inside me collapsed, as if a scyth had shaved my reason and memory, cutting through all the ideas, reflections, and knowledge that I'd managed to accumulate. An emptiness opened up inside me, I was consumed by an inner desolation, a sudden fit of idiocy – something within me refused to comprehend, my mind could contain neither the extent of the evil committed nor the immensity of suffering endured in that place. That very stark, very silent place, like the outstretched palm of a dead body lying on the ground, with its face to the sky. An even starker, more silent sky. There are exiles who, when at last they return to their country, go down on their knees to kiss the soil of their regained homeland. There, within the space of a single moment, I felt banished for ever from the land of men and suddenly brought back again to this same land, and I would indeed have fallen to my knees, but not to kiss the soil, rather to bang my forehead on the ground and beat my fists against it. And ground and sky were one, a poor drumskin devoid of resonance. There was a time when God brought assassins and perjurors to account. But there, he said nothing. A great deal has been said about this silence, about the scandal of this failure to speak out, and the scandal of those contemporaries of the massacre who knew what was going on, but didn't have the courage, or the intelligence, or the heart to act on it. It's easy for us to condemn all those crimes committed in the past, to denounce that dual silence, vertical and horizontal, which left the executioners free to do whatever they wanted, and carried to an extreme the suffering of the victims, abandoned on all sides. It is much more problematic to content ourselves with a powerless lament in the face of the countless crimes that are currently being committed. Yet that is what we are doing, however great and sorrowful our indignation. All I personally can do is utter an inward cry, directed to myself from myself, in a pitiful laceration of conscience. As for God, I can only register the cold tenacity of His silence, but I don't know whether, beyond that silence, He is aggrieved and groans in the depths of His conscience.

'At Birkenau, the executioners planted poplars round the camp, because these trees grow fast and high, and screen against prying eyes. The poplars are still there, very slender and quivering. They stand on the edge of that hell created by the hands of men to torture other men, like the nymph Leuca, transformed into a poplar by the god of the dead and planted by him at the gates of underworld. The poplars of Birkenau, which the executioners wanted to recruit to their cause, have never shared in that contemptible complicity, and they testify with absolute discretion on behalf of the victims of whom nothing remains – nothing but their never-to-be-consoled suffering. These funerary trees perpetuate the silence that enclosed this place, and denounce the silence of a humanity that lost its soul, just as much as that of a God who showed no mercy. They marry legend, which turned them into trees associated with grief, death and tears, with history, which set them in the margins of one of its darkest pages.

'Will you have a little more coffee?'

Ludvik put his cup down on the edge of the counter. He was frozen to the marrow, but no longer thinking of getting away. Something now detained him. What this man had just been saying corresponded exactly with what he himself had experienced when he went to Auschwitz-Birkenau, some fifteen years ago, too. The poplars that trembled in the nihilistic desolation of that place, like the inconsolable Heliades after the death of their brother Phaeton, who plunged from the sky, his body in flames.

The vendor poured him some coffee and continued his monologue.

'But now I have a confession to make: after that visit, which as a rule leaves anyone who has the least conscience and sensitivity without an appetite, at least for the rest of the day, well, I felt terribly hungry. I came back to the town of Auschwitz, I went into a restaurant and ordered a meal. I still remember it: pork with cabbage. And then a dessert. And as soon as I came out of the restaurant, I went in search of another, and I ordered another meal. More pork, and potatoes, and another dessert. I was still ravenous, with an insatiable hunger. I went into a third restaurant, and again I gave free rein to my compulsive hunger. Fish, this time. I had to eat, chew, swallow. Until I was full to bursting, to the point of nausea.'

He broke off to roll a cigarette.

'And afterwards?' asked Ludvik, who was aware of having had exactly the same reaction, down to the smallest detail, on the day of his visit to the two camps.

'Afterwards? Well, I was sick, of course! I had to hurry to get off the bus that was taking me to the station, I felt so much like vomiting.'

'I meant, after that, in the days and weeks that followed,' Ludvik corrected himself, remembering his own rush to get off the bus and his pitiful retching.

'Oh, after that . . . nothing in particular. A sense of unease, of mental anguish, but it wasn't long before time suppressed them. Everyday life reclaimed its rights, with its little worries, pleasures and vexations, tasks and obligations, and also with the pseudo problems with which all of us have the knack of enriching our banal lives.'

'But why are you telling me all this?'

'Why?' said the vendor, spreading his hands like someone hazarding a reply. 'To cheat the boredom, probably. There's no worse ill than boredom, which stealthily, while seemingly innocuous, demoralizes us and detaches us from everything, from others, from ourselves. It's a blight as insidious as it is voracious that gradually eats away the heart's and mind's intelligence, it consumes our memory so that in the end all that's left of it are a few small islands of obdurate recollections, like tumours and warts – such being the sorrows of love, for example. And this corrupts your vision; you lose sight of what matters, and what you continue to see is then very often distorted, or blurred, or seen through one eye only.'

He crushed his empty cup in one hand, and tossed it out through the kiosk hatch. The discarded cup rolled on the pavement. 'There,' he concluded in an abruptly sharp tone of voice. 'Let it be cast out and trampled underfoot like salt that has lost its savour!'

Ludvik looked at the vendor with a certain amazement, then, still prey to his sudden fit of anger, the man exclaimed, 'Yes, cursed be the man whose heart is caught in the toils of boredom! For he shall be like the heath in the desert: and shall not see when good cometh, but shall inhabit the parched places in the wilderness, in a salt land and not inhabited.'

And with this fiery quotation from Jeremiah, he abruptly brought down the corrugated-iron shutter over his hatch. As much taken aback as he was irritated by this behaviour, Ludvik banged against the shutter, shouting, 'Open up!'

'Too late, I'm closed!' replied the vendor in a gloomy voice. 'Go and buy your paper elsewhere.'

'It's not just the paper, I've got some questions I want to ask you.'

'Bah! Ask yourself.'

Ludvik knocked on the shutter again. 'Please, open up!'

But the man did not stir. Indeed, there was not the slightest sound from inside the kiosk. Ludvik persisted for a while longer, but to no effect. Eventually tiring of this, he went off, shrugging his shoulders. 'Silly old fool!' he hissed between his teeth.

The very next day, however, Ludvik returned to the kiosk. The various incidents that had occurred over the past few months had each in its own way to a greater or lesser degree astonished or annoyed him, but none had intrigued him as much as this newspaper vendor who did not bother, and even refused, to sell his merchandise, preferring to hold forth at length, offering cigarettes and coffee the more easily to detain any passer-by. This little strategem was quite harmless in itself: an old man is bored and freezing in his kiosk, waiting for custom, and when at last someone stops to buy a paper, he takes the opportunity to buttonhole him and relieve his solitude for a while. The art of stealing a chance to talk to someone when old age and life have made you an outcast. Ludvik could understand this, the town was rife with such people deprived of the spoken word. It was the tenor of the man's remarks, and especially their insidious nature, that disturbed Ludvik, for he had reflected on everything the man told him, and he remained unnerved by some points of very close resemblance between the newspaper vendor's recollections and his own. He would like to have questioned him in more detail on this subject. And furthermore he could not explain the man's abrupt change in behaviour, who had switched from friendliness to hatefulness without any warning or apparent reason, a little like that young idiot with the salt rose. And the vendor also had an obsession with salt, like all those other nutcases whose whimsicalities he had had to endure.

Because of this guy ensconced in his niche like a bust, Ludvik had been virtually unable to sleep, and he could have been sleepwalking when he made his way back up Korunni Street to the kiosk. But when he reached it, he definitely felt he was having a bad dream. Could months have gone by in the space of a single night? The kiosk was in an advanced state of rack and ruin. There it stood on the pavement, all rickety, covered with frozen birdshit, plastered with torn old posters and advertisements that had become illegible. A few words were written in chalk on the now rusted and extremely dented shutter over the hatch. Ludvik had difficulty in deciphering these words. 'But Lot's wife looked back, and she was turned into a pillar of salt.'

Ludvik felt as if he had turned into a pillar of ice through amazement, then a pillar of fire through exasperation, which overcame him almost immediately. He gave the kiosk a violent kick, and went storming off. In his anger he fulminated incoherently, not even knowing against whom he was raging – himself, the vendor, the other lunatics, biblical quotations, then, by extension, he also cursed Eva, who was no better, with her sphinx-like affectations on the phone; his publisher, who was sure never to pay him; and, while he was at it, the author of the book that he had struggled so much to translate. At this point, he paused in the crescendo of his bad-temperedness. He dared not rail against the Great Rabbi Loew. But since he had some grousing in reserve, he searched for some other fool to berate mentally, and he routed out from some forgotten corner of his bitterness the uncivilized person who had pinched his raincoat on the train. He cast around further among his acquaintances, but came up with no one. The snowball of his bad-temperedness thus came to its natural end, and soon began to melt away. All that he was left with was a sense of confusion and tiredness. Moreover, he felt feverish. When he got home he made himself a toddy, had a hot bath, and went back to bed.

He slept all afternoon, in deep, clammy slumber, and when he woke up, late in the evening, he was drenched in sweat and shivering. Failing to find the vendor, he had instead caught a serious bout of flu. He got up and went to the kitchen to make himself another toddy with a much bigger dose of rum than of the sugared water he mixed with it. He downed it with three aspirins. Then he went back to bed where he sank into an even more torpid sleep. At dawn he began to toss and turn, crowded fragments of dreams flashed through his mind. It was one of these dreams that woke him with a start. A fat woman in a shawl and starched skirt, puffed out like an umbrella, was skating very fast and erratically on a frozen river. While attempting to pirouette, she slipped, and having spun round, balanced on one foot like an enormous top, she came crashing down onto the ice, which broke; then, as the plump skater sank like a stone, multicolour banderoles streamed out from her petticoats and flapped in the sky, cracking like whips. All this created such a racket that Ludvik started up, in his bed. He shook his head, rubbed his eyes and gradually recovered his senses, and suddenly burst out laughing.

'Fat Ludmilla!' he exclaimed. And he told himself that he was quite wrong to worry about supposed mysteries that could undoubtedly be explained by a similarly naive and ridiculous piece of deception as that of the funerary ribbons that went missing only to decorate the petticoats of one who had a love of finery and slightly macabre tastes.

'Ah, good old Ludmilla!' thought Ludvik, getting out of bed. 'Every time I remember her silly story, it puts everything back into proportion. The next time I have the misfortune to meet some crackpot whose brain is pickled in brine, I shall summon her and her petticoats, to come my rescue.' And he already felt much better.

During the day he took another excellent decision: to go to the mountains for a week, to get a change of air and give his mind a rest, after which he would settle down to work again. He went to a travel agency and booked a train ticket for the day after next, and a room, at an inn, in a village in the Tatras.

On the eve of his departure he rang Eva for news of Brum. She too had caught a cold, her voice was hoarse. She said that the physical decline was following its course, that her uncle's emaciated body was increasingly covered with bed sores, and that the doctors' were now talking of 'the Brum case'. She also intimated at the end of the conversation that it would not be long before this ordeal was over. Refusing to comfort Eva while she persisted in making such Delphic utterances, Ludvik therefore did not ask her to be any more precise about the probable date of Brum's death, which slightly vexed him after all, now that he was going to be away. But he reassured himself with the thought that a week was not a very long time, and he could always make another phone call during his stay in the mountains. He closed his suitcase, into which he crammed a few volumes along with his notebook.

The journey lasted all night, then he had to catch a bus that made alarmingly heavy weather of going uphill. At last he was rewarded for his long and uncomfortable trek by the sight of the village where he was to stay.

A very high village perched amid silence, set against the blue of the sky. And all the countryside round about was transformed by the snow into a sparkling desert, a region of dreams and patience. The village and the land kept their history silent, they huddled in waiting, waiting that extended far beyond expectation of the arrival of the next season, which was also engraved in them, of course, but without urgency or nostalgia. It was a much more expansive waiting, completely stark, without object or impetuosity. A solitary waiting, imbued with slowness, meekness, severity. A waiting in which were joined the blue of the sky and the basalt blackness of the nights, the wandering of the clouds and their shadows on the ground, the shimmering of the stars, the memory of the elements beneath the rock and outer surface, the warm breath of the beasts, and the gaze of men resting on this silence, as well as the flight of birds passing through all these things.

What struck Ludvik was the smell of snow, for here it had a smell, and the cold had a taste. His inn was situated a little above the village, and he had to climb up a road edged with rosy-tinted snowdrifts. The façade of the inn, was round and all made of wood, in imitation of an enormous barrel: a house straight out of a fairy tale or the imagination of a heavy drinker. A young girl was drying glasses behind the counter when he entered the place. He introduced himself and said that he had booked a room. The girl stared at him boldly. She had big black eyes and a beauty spot at the base of her neck. She put down her glass and her cloth and announced that she was going to fetch the landlady. She had no sooner gone than a piercing cry rang out from a staircase at the back of the room. 'Coming aboard!' And almost immediately a cannonball came hurtling down the stairs. It landed with a terrible crash on the parquet floor and burst into sobs. It was a child of about five years old. In one hand he held a plastic yellow sabre, which was all twisted, and with the other, clenched in a fist, he was rubbing his eyes. Ludvik went over to him, but the kid howled more than ever. The young girl came running and crouched down by the child, whom she picked up in her arms. 'Now, haven't I told you a hundred times not to jump like that from the top of the stairs . . .'

'It's his fault!' cried the youngster, pointing a vengeful finger in Ludvik's direction.

'He wasn't to know . . .'

'Yes! He should have caught me, so there!'

A third person finally appeared on the scene, the landlady. She was a woman of about sixty, with grizzly hair tied back in a heavy bun, and a pear-shaped body. She wore a brick-red dress and a big flowered shawl, and thick sock-type slippers. She rolled like a bear as she walked.

'So, young cabin boy, you fell from the rigging?' She had an extraordinarily deep voice.

The young girl carried away the sniffling child, who stuck his tongue out at Ludvik over the girl's shoulder.

'He thought it was one of the regulars down here,' the woman explained, 'they know that when the boy shouts, "Coming aboard!", he hurls himself from the landing and expects someone to catch him in the air. It's a game he likes to play. And so do they.'

Then she showed him round and took him to his room. She told him what time dinner and breakfast were served, but said he could also have them brought to his room if he wanted.

He went out for a walk. In the evening he dined in the main room, where he lingered after the last customers had gone. He was reading the paper when he heard a whispered: 'Hey, pst! Coming aboard!' Then there was a creaking of stairs beneath a pitter-patter of footsteps. Ludvik rushed to the bottom of the staircase and a moment later the child dropped into his arms. This time he broke into a radiant smile. Ludvik put him down, and the child pulled up his pyjama bottoms, while jigging around.

'Aren't you in bed yet?' asked Ludvik.

'Yes, but shh!' and he put his index finger to his lips.

Ludvik noticed that his fingernail was all black. The child explained that he had hurt himself, banging it by mistake with a hammer while building a model boat. But when Ludvik was gauche enough to ask if the boy wanted to be a sailor when he grew up, the youngster shrugged his shoulders scornfully and replied, 'Are you crazy? I want to be a pirate!' Then he added with pride, 'And my ship will be called the *Lubosek*!' Thus introducing himself, by hoisting his colours on the pirate ship, he once again pulled his pyjamas up to his navel and climbed back upstairs on tiptoe.

Ludvik soon followed. He went to bed early by comparison with the hours he usually kept. After a bad night on the train the night before, then his long walk in the snow that afternoon, he felt a kind of tiredness whose pleasure had been lost to him: a tiredness that was all mellowness, pervasive and soothing, such as one experiences in childhood after a day spent playing in the open air, such as one experiences, too, after hours of lovemaking and sensual pleasure in the consummation of desire, when that desire is rooted deep in a love well watered with wonder, tenderness and joy.

He woke in the middle of the night in a room whose smell, silence and dimensions were unfamiliar to him, and with a brute, physical sensation of loneliness. He remained for a few moments lying in bed, his eyes wide open in the dark, then order returned to his thoughts. He got up to go to the bathroom, pulled on his socks, his trousers and a pullover, and went out into the corridor, but unable to find the light switch, he was left groping in the dark. He went up and down the corridor twice, unable to find the right door. Feeling his way along the wall, his hand met with empty space. He concluded that he was on the landing of the staircase leading to the room below, and he descended the steps cautiously. He would be better able to orientate himself downstairs and he knew where the ground-floor toilets were. But suddenly the wall went round a corner, and Ludvik stumbled; he only just recovered his balance. He realized that he was on a different staircase, however he continued to descend, for a glow of light was finally discernible. He came into a dimly lit room with a monumental pear enthroned in the centre of it. A woman sat there, motionless, on a wooden stool. She had her back to Ludvik. She was dressed in a white cotton nightgown, tinged pale yellow by the lighting. A thick brown braid threaded with white snaked down her back, emphasizing the curve of a generous behind.

'Is that you, little cabin boy?' asked the woman without turning round.

Ludvik recognized the landlady and stammered out his apologies.

'Oh, it's you,' she said, 'I was afraid it was the boy, he sometimes has nightmares that wake him up. As for the house, it's inevitable that you'll get lost when you're not familiar with it. The façade's barrel-shaped, but inside it's as full of bends and twists as a still. You see that low door on the left, that's where the toilets are. Be careful, there are two steps.'

Ludvik slipped into the bathroom. When he came out again, the woman called out to him.

'Do you suffer from insomnia too? If you feel like killing time until you feel sleepy again, you can keep me company for a while. Sit down here. There are some cigarettes on the table beside you.'

Ludvik installed himself on a little sofa covered with a faded green, woollen plush fabric. He was facing the woman and noticed that she was bathing her feet.

'Funny spectacle, hey?' she said smiling. 'But I have a lot of trouble with my feet, because I have bad circulation, and it often wakes me up at night, so I soak them for a little while in a bowl of hot water. I add a drop of eucalyptus oil, because I like the smell. Would you be an angel and light me a cigarette.'

As she smoked, she threw back her head with every exhalation. Ludvik asked her some questions about the village, and about the inn.

'There's not much to say about the village, or maybe there's a lot, it depends. Like everywhere else, it has its wise folk and its fools, its good souls and bad, its share of golden hours and of misfortune. As for this barrel of an inn, it was my husband's idea. A barrel! It's certainly in his own image – a wretched drunk! He even asked to be buried with a bottle of brandy in his coffin. And he was.'

'Was it a long time ago that he died?'

'Just before the child was born; they wouldn't have had time to get to know each other. But seeing he didn't care a damn about the little bastards he left behind him all over the place, it didn't make a lot of difference. Except that with this last child that he fathered, the mother came and dumped him on me one fine day when he was seven months old, then she disappeared and there's never been any sign of her since. And so much the better.'

She wiggled her toes in the bowl a little. 'The water's got cold, I must add some more hot.' She rose heavily from her seat and went over to a stove on which there were two kettles standing. Her buttocks heaved under her nightgown. She touched the outside of one of the two kettles, decided that the water was still quite warm, came back and poured it into the bowl. Her wet feet left temporary imprints on the orange-coloured linoleum. She opened a little glass phial and tipped it over the bowl: three oily rings formed on top of the water, then became diluted in it, releasing a strong smell of eucalyptus. She sat down again, breathing heavily, and reimmersed her feet.

'Ivo was a real drunkard,' she resumed, 'but that said, I knew what I was letting myself in for. The day he proposed to me, he was completely drunk. He came to my house, asked me to go out into the courtyard with him because he had something important to tell me. I followed him, he was reeling. Outside, it was all covered with snow, just like it is now. Then he planted himself two feet in front of me, with his back turned, opened his flies, and pissed on the snow. But he didn't piss any old how, he wrote my name in the snow: "Vladimira, I love you." The snow was all pitted with the letters he had traced out, just like that, in a single stream, and they were edged with steam. It was not without style, as well as vulgarity. And there was even a spelling mistake. Ivo never had any idea how to spell.'

'And after this declaration?'

'He buttoned up his flies, turned to me and asked me to marry him. I told him to come back the next morning. If the declaration he had just written survived till then, and the wind didn't blow it away during the night, and the snow didn't melt, then the answer would be yes. The next day he came back, we went out into the courtyard, the snow had lasted, the words were still perfectly legible. We were married the following spring. He was dead drunk on our wedding night, of course, and he got taken with a peculiar fancy: he collected up the bouquets of flowers and decided to make a fricassé with them, so he tore off the flowerheads and threw them into a big frying pan which he cooked over a high flame. He never got over this fad: whenever he was completely plastered he would rush for the frying pan to cook up whatever he could lay his hands on. One day it was his slippers, another the alarm clock. It's a miracle he never set fire to the house, this barrel's entirely made of wood. Anyway, it was because of this mania for throwing everything into a frying pan that he died.'

'Sautéeing a bomb?'

'Not at all. He drowned. It was an autumn night,

it was already very cold. He'd been carousing with two of his mates who were just as drunk as he was. On the way back they passed the pond on the outskirts of the village, and he noticed a swan gliding on the water. Well, he cried out that he was going to wring the neck of that fine feathered bugger, and cook him in his frying pan. He took off his clothes and, in his socks and underpants, dived into the pond, bellowing. The water was freezing. Ivo hadn't swum three strokes when he sank to the bottom like a stone. They didn't fish out his body until the next day. The swan was still there, parading on the water, all white, the whiteness of oblivion, indifference. I'd liked to have caught him, wrung his long neck, and tied it into a knot like the one on St Nicholas's crook, and then plucked him. Feather by feather. But what happened was the opposite, he wrung my neck, and plucked my heart. Ah, what a character!'

'What do you mean?'

'Pah! That's enough for this evening. It's already after four. It would be a good idea to get a little sleep, don't you think?'

And Vladimira took her reddened feet out of the bowl, dried them with a towel and pulled on thick woollen socks. Ludvik stood up, and wished her goodnight.

'What's left of the night,' sighed Vladimira. 'I have to be up again in less than two hours. Never mind. Anyway, now that you know the way, if you ever have any more trouble sleeping at night, don't hesitate to come and join me at the bottom of my barrel.'

*

The next morning the sky was overcast. Ludvik stayed in his room, where he read and leafed through his notebook. He noticed that he had twice made a note of the same event, several pages apart, dating it differently. On one page he had even transcribed a short extract from the work that gave an account of this event: it was a book called *Zemah David* by David Gans. He reread this passage.

'By an act of grace and in a desire for truth, our sovereign lord Emperor Rudolf, just Sire, source of brilliant and glorious light, may His Majesty be exalted, summoned to his presence the Gaon, our Master Rabbi Loew Ben Bezalel, and received him with the utmost benevolence, entering into conversation with him, as one speaking to his equal. As for the essence and import of their exchange, these remain a mystery on which the two men have placed the seal of secrecy. The event took place in Prague, on Sunday, 3rd Adar 5352.'

On the other page, he noted this meeting again, but dating it 10th Adar 5352, according to another account. This slight disparity was basically of little importance, what bothered Ludvik was more the fact that he did not really know how to translate these dates precisely into the Christian calendar. Nor could he remember why he had mentioned this event twice. Because of the significance that chroniclers of the time attributed to it, undoubtedly, and because of the eminent role the Maharal had played in this meeting suffused with mystery and invested with a Messianic dimension, since it brought immense hope. That of a reconciliation between the Christian world and the scattered tribes of Israel, and the promise, therefore, of an end to the sufferings endured by this people. But the seal of secrecy had remained unbroken on the tenor of this dialogue, and history soon reduced to ashes and tears of blood the fine hope momentarily raised thanks to two men daring to speak to each other face to face, with their hearts open to the infinite and to the disturbing murmur of the world that rose from the depths of the ages, constantly wavering between song, cry and silence.

In the early afternoon the sun pierced the mist. Ludvik went out for a walk. And there was the same dazzling snow as when he arrived. Just as before, earth, sky, water and trees held their breath, silenced their voices.

Ludvik thought of Vladimira sitting at night, at the bottom of her barrel, delivering her speech to restore a little sap to her past, a little life to her deceased husband. The pond where he drowned one autumn evening lay very nearby, its frozen waters forming a broad bluish oval like a closed eyelid. Beneath that eyelid of ice, no memory, no concern for him who had met his death there. Remembrance and anguish fell only to those left behind, who with the passage of time transformed their memories into legends.

He thought too of the old newspaper vendor confined in his kiosk, raving in a memory much vaster than himself, much too far-reaching and cruel for him. He pictured the ramshackle kiosk, all begrimed with dirty snow, the muddy, sooty snow of the city. And suddenly a vision of the three Magi came back to him. The three figures in brown and grey, bent against the wind, walking through an ashen wilderness, each clutching a bowl in his hands. And immediately the image was replicated in its negative version: the three ivory-coloured figures, similarly bowed and straining to make headway against a strong milky wind. The two visions came in close succession, but not on top of each other, so that not only were their colour tones reversed but also the direction of their progress. And again this slow haunting image, by a process of association he could not explain to himself, reminded him of Brum.

Brum: Ludvik had never thought so much about him since that last visit he paid, as if that visit, after eleven years' absence and relative oblivion, had concluded the process of effacement of the great Brum, to be replaced by the reduced and pathetic old man in his silent struggle with death. But were these vague memories that kept resurfacing in his mind truly an act of thought? It was more a passive kind of thought, with the unexpected incursion, here and there, of a flash of reverie, a subtle disquiet, a start of amazement, like the resurgent image of the three Magi. Maybe when someone who is, or was, close to us, to a greater or lesser degree, is in the process of dying, then something radiates from that person to their nearest and dearest, something indefinable, untangible – an obscure glow, a silence rustling with whispers, a sense of intense cold and tenderness. As if the ever more muted, ever more slow and painful beating of a heart about to depart was secretly echoed in the then alerted hearts of others.

Ludvik walked along the frosty paths, and the space all around him extended its whiteness as far as the eye could see, the wind blew so cold he could hardly breathe, isolating him even more in his passive thoughts.

'Now where did we get to?' asked Vladimira, who had put on a green-and-black-chequered robe over her nightgown for modesty's sake, in anticipation of another nocturnal visit from her guest.

'The swan that plucked your heart,' said Ludvik, settling down again on the sofa.

'Ah, yes, that wretched fowl . . . For days, weeks, I kept going back to the edge of the pond, I would plant myself on the spot where Ivo jumped in and plunged to his death, and there I would watch the swan gliding on the water. Backwards and forwards, backwards and forwards, sowing questions in my mind – or I might say, leaving my mind riddled with questions. For I asked myself questions as never before. Why this? And why that? What is the meaning of life? What does it mean to die? What are we doing here on this earth? Is there a God, or isn't there? And so on and so forth. In short, the complete arsenal of doubts that everyone drags round with them, but which it had never occurred to me to consider. And I didn't find any answers, or rather I did, but the answers always came in pairs, which were contradictory. So I kept coming back to where I started from. And there was one silly question, a very silly question, that haunted me more than any other. I wondered whether I had loved Ivo, if I had ever loved anybody, in fact. And then, what does it mean, to love? My heart felt so empty, so raw. I would stare at people, straight in the eye, as if I was trying to delve into their flesh, right down to their entrails, to see what was inside them, to see if they knew what love was. The result was, people lowered their eyes, they looked away, they said I had a brutal gaze. I sent clients fleeing, I ruined their appetite for eating and drinking. But it was much worse for me. It ruined my appetite for living. I couldn't sleep any more. At night I could still see the swan with its neck in the shape of a question mark.'

'Did you find the answer in the end?'

'Let's say, the answer found me. And it was not so much an answer as a constant urgency, I just had to behave as if I had solved the problem. It was when that girl came and left me holding her bastard child in my arms: a few kilos of flesh, nerves, smiles and tears. The po-faced swan flew out of my mind, and the child took his place. Maybe, love is quite simply taking others just as they come to us, and caring for them as much as they need, without grumbling about it, without expecting anything particular in return. Love isn't some idea that we may have about it, it lies in actions carried out from day to day. I'd got it all wrong in the questions I'd been asking myself on the edge of the pond, especially the ones about Ivo, because the time to love people is when they're alive, not afterwards, when it's all over. Don't you think so?'

This question thrown out by Vladimira in the course

of their night-time conversation remained for a long time suspended in Ludvik's mind. Had he loved Esther? Yes, passionately. But was passion not misguided love? Seemingly so, since there was the expectation of something in return – total unshared possession of the loved one. It was necessary to dig deep beneath the excesses, delusions, contradictions and violence of passion to uncover a little true love. Sometimes there was none to be found. Ludvik, searched, dug out, explored, scoured every corner of his memory, heart, conscience. Jealousy, anger, loathing, bitterness still overlay his memory of Esther, he still could not think about her without experiencing a painful emotion – a mixture of bewilderment and sour distress. But he did not give up, he burrowed beneath all this debris, these cinders, this dross, and suddenly he felt he was holding Esther's face in his bare hands. Not just the face of his lover, but her face, the face of a human individual, unique among the multitude of other unique beings. Her face, as naked, as vulnerable as his own hands that were overcome only with tenderness, unguarded and unrestrained. Her face, like fresh water in the hollow of his palms, in the middle of the desert. And he knew that he had loved her, loved her much more than with mere passion, much more than he had suspected. He realized that he had loved her to a point of no-return. Then for the first time, all anger and bitterness fell away from him. The beauty of having loved her, and his gratitude for having loved her, proved such that in his broken heart all resentment was cast aside. His heart was still broken, but like a wounded animal, drained with exhaustion, that might lie down on the threshold of wondrousness, and wait there, without whining or snarling, expecting nothing.

The next night he did not go down into the low-ceilinged room, redolent of eucalyptus, where Vladimira relieved her aching feet in the lustral waters of a ceramic bowl. He stayed in his room, lying on his bed, with a book in his hands, but with his eyes more often raised towards the bare wall than resting on the pages. His distractedness went hand in hand with a strange attentiveness; he felt required to keep vigil, but without being able to apprehend what it was he was waiting for. He fell asleep like this, completely dressed, the book dropped in his lap, the light on. The same thing happened the next day, and the day after that. All day he would roam the white paths, without any particular objective: paths of no significance, that led nowhere. A labyrinth out in the open, vibrant with cold and light, where from time to time the wind blew, the wind growled, a branch cracked in the distance, or the harsh cry of a bird rang out as though to heighten the silence all the more. His gaze cleaved to the snow, his ears to the barren silence, and his thoughts to the emptiness. Sometimes, for no more than the batting of an eyelid, he would glimpse the procession of the Magi floating on the horizon, in a slight dazzlement. He would return at nightfall, numb with cold, with solitude, completely permeated with spaciousness and whiteness.

He dined early, played a few games of cards with

customers at the bar. The child would run between the tables, sometimes he would creep underneath one of them and stay there, crouched on the floor, listening to the players rambling on. The young waitress, Pavlinka, would drive him out of his hiding place, as though chasing a little kitten, then the child would run away laughing, rush upstairs and then throw himself down the staircase uttering his ritual cry.

One evening when Ludvik had just caught him in midair, Lubosek, staring him straight in the eye, and in a voice breathless from running about, said to him, 'Why do all the others talk, the whole time, and you don't say anything?'

'I prefer to listen,' replied Ludvik.

'I like listening too. So don't you know any stories?'

'Yes, I do, and tomorrow, if you like, I'll tell you one,' Ludvik promised as he put him down on the floor.

'Which story?'

'The story of Moby Dick.'

'Who's Moby Dick?'

'A huge and white whale, like the mountains here.'

'And what does the whale do?'

'It lives in the ocean, that's as the big the sky is here. And it fights.'

'Who does it fight?'

'Captain Ahab.'

'And how big is he?'

'As big as a man can be on the open sea, with a

heart as violent as the storms, and a leg made of whale bone.'

At these words, the child's eyes widened with admiration, but Vladimira called him and took him off to bed, and he did not find out any more until the next morning.

On his last evening Ludvik went down to pay a farewell visit to Vladimira. A brightly-flowered shawl was wrapped round her shoulders. She was sitting not on the stool but in an armchair, and she was not bathing her feet.

'I've been expecting you,' she said. 'You're leaving early tomorrow, but you'll keep me company for a little while, won't you?'

Ludvik kept her company for a long while, listening to her lovely deep voice. She talked sensibly, with simplicity, and always in the same even tone. She did not judge people, she only appraised the weight of their presence in the world, and the degree of kindness in their hearts. It was not her concern to pontificate about good and bad. Ludvik also noticed that not once did she express any complaint or regret.

When he went back upstairs he found the little boy, huddled on a step in the angle of the staircase. He was asleep. Ludvik hesitated to go down and tell Vladimira, because she had just retired to her room. He picked the child up in his arms, without waking him, and carried him up to the landing. But he did not know which was his room, so he put the boy in his own bed, beside him.

The child's breathing was very regular, and deep.

Ludvik listened to this breathing with the same denuded attention as he had brought to his long rambles in the snow. He listened as one does approaching the sea, on hearing the low murmur of the waters retelling their tales over and over again, without beginning or end, as one does on the edge of the forest when a far-reaching rustle runs through the branches. The voice of the most extreme outdoors and of the most intimate inwardness. In counterpoint to the child's breathing, the wind moaned loudly. It was a long musical phrase, of total simplicity, with a hypnotic theme, and of austere beauty. The child, the wind, one same breathing at two pitches, two speeds; the fragile, the powerful, a singular mystery blazing a trail across the earth.

At the end of these few days of calm Ludvik suddenly felt an obscure disquiet welling up again inside him, without reason and without object. A sense of anxiety and a sense of the unknown, as if instead of soon making his way to the station to return home, he was going to set off alone, with no luggage, or map, or compass, to smuggle himself across a very indefinite border. Nevertheless he fell asleep; a short windblown sleep. No dream could develop, no image settle, the wind was blowing too hard, unceasingly, blowing away everything, levelling everything. It even blew away the vision of the three Magi. Three lengths of pale fabric tumbling helter-skelter across the earth's surface, flush with the sky.

When he got up, the child was still sleeping. Vladimira was already in the room downstairs. They had coffee together. He told her how he had found the child on the stairs and had put him in his own bed.

'His father invented a house in the shape of a barrel, and he persists in thinking of it as a ship sailing an imaginary ocean. This room is the main deck, the landing is the upper deck, my bedroom is the hold and the attic the crow's nest, the customers are a horde of pirates and Pavlinka is sometimes a seagull and sometimes a dolphin. As for me, he's given me the leading role, as the figurehead! Those waves had better watch out! But I think he was about to name you captain. Your story about the whale fired his imagination. He's going to miss you. If you found him on the stairs, that's surely because he was looking for you. He'll be happy to wake up in the captain's cabin, but sad that you've gone.'

Outside the wind's shrill whistle still sounded. For the last time Ludvik descended the narrow path banked with hardened snow the colour of pink quartz and milky white. The light was just coming over the mountaintops and already driving the mist back down into the valleys. As he walked, he paid even closer attention to the landscape than on previous days. He breathed in the empty expanse, the cold's very bare skin. The snow exhaled at once its smell, its whiteness and its silence. Time was as though suspended, a concentrated dose of emptiness, of timelessness, breaching the sound of duration, interrupting its flow.

He suddenly saw at some distance a small, plum-coloured figure, standing motionless by the side of the road. As he drew nearer, he saw that it was a child of about eight years old, wearing a purple anorak and a light grey woollen hat pulled right down to the eyebrows. The child was slightly hunched forward and slowly turned its head from left to right as if inspecting all around. The hat had a long braided woollen tassel that tufted out at the end. Whenever the child moved its head the tassel swung like a pendulum. Ludvik could not really tell whether the child was a girl or a boy, but so intensely was it scanning the ground he thought the child must be looking for something that meant a lot to it.

'Have you lost something?' he asked.

The child abruptly straightened up and darted a solemn gaze at him from under his hat, then by way of reply, blurted out, 'Have you?'

It was a little boy, with very dark blue eyes. He looked so aggressive, like Lubosek that first evening after his unfortunate tumble to bottom of the stairs, that Ludvik burst out laughing.

'Don't laugh so loudly,' said the boy drily, 'you'll chase away the birds' shadows.'

'Shadows?' said Ludvik, taken by surprise. 'And they're frightened of laughter?'

'They're not frightened of anything, or anybody, but they don't like noise.'

He had already turned away and was not taking the slightest notice of Ludvik. He was examining the ground again. He stuck one hand in his pocket and pulled out a handful of grain that he threw on to the snow, in the direction of a passing bird's shadow. And the shadow stopped for a moment. Ludvik looked up, and saw a rook that remained suspended in the air directly above its shadow. Then the little boy scattered another handful of grain on the shadow of another rook and the same curious thing happened.

'What are you doing?'

'Can't you see? I'm feeding the birds' shadows.'

'What gave you that idea! It's the birds of flesh and feather that are hungry, not their shadows.'

'I know,' said the child, who nonetheless continued to feed his phantom birds.

Ludvik then noticed that the grains he threw did not rest on the snow but immediately disappeared into it, as if they melted on contact with it, and tiny holes were sunk wherever they fell. The birds' shadows were all pitted, as if he had riddled them with crumbs of metal shot or fiery pellets of grain.

'What exactly is that birdfood you're throwing at them? It seems very acidic.'

The answer shot back, as acid as the birdfood. 'It's salt.'

At this word, Ludvik started, but he recalled that silly story young children are told, that it's possible to catch birds by pouring salt on their tails. The boy was still young enough to believe such nonsense, and thus reassured, Ludvik joined in the game.

'Salt? What a good idea! And have you already captured many birds' shadows using this method?'

The little bird-catcher did not even deign to reply to this idiotic question, he contented himself with casting a severe glance at Ludvik, then, his supply of salt exhausted, he remained motionless, his arms dangling. His lips and fingernails were blue with cold.

Ludvik dared not ask any more questions. He felt slightly ridiculous and evidently this fractious child preferred to be alone. So he was about to walk away when the child began to talk.

'Capture! What an ugly word, so stupid! The things you say are like your laughter – noise, nothing but noise.' The child had uttered these words in a subdued voice, without anger or scorn, with sadness rather, and Ludvik was disturbed, even touched, by this note of sadness. So,far from scolding the insolent child, he too spoke gently.

'All right, I'll keep quiet, anyway I have to go, but before I do, I'd like you to tell me what you think about when you throw salt on the birds' shadows.'

The child breathed deeply, then, gazing raptly into the white vastness, he replied almost under his breath, 'These shadows are like the brilliance of stars in the darkness, the reflections of clouds on the fields, the smiles of people you love, you can't catch them but you can enter into alliance with them, promise them – promise yourself – never to forget them. Friendship isn't only reserved for people, you can also be friends, in simplicity and kindness, with plants, trees, the light, stones, the wind and all the elements, with things, with every passing thing of beauty. When you say that you're friends with someone, or something, you make a pact of loyalty, honesty and respect. Salt is offered as a symbol of welcome and hospitality. Well, I scatter it over everything I love as a gesture of welcome into my memory, of invitation into my heart.'

Ludvik was so amazed by these words that he

could not help expressing his surprise. 'But who are you? You don't talk like boys of your age . . . What's your name?'

The child abruptly turned towards him and confronted him with the expression of a little ruffian spoiling for a fight, and he shouted rather than spoke, 'What does it matter to you what my name is? What on earth do you care, who I am and what I'm called, eh? And how would you know whether or not I talk like boys of my age? I talk the way you used to talk when you were my age, but you've forgotten that, you've forgotten everything, you've let everything lose its flavour, you've let the salt of your memory turn yellow, and the salt of your vows of friendship with the world, with people, become tainted. Bah!' He shook his head, pursed his mauve lips and turned away. He took a few steps, bent over a bush that formed a white cupola on the edge of the bank, and pulled out from beneath its snowy branches a little wooden toboggan and hopped onto it.

'Wait!' said Ludvik, starting to make a move, a gesture, but suddenly his throat felt so constricted that all that came out was a raucous breath, and his body so aching with cold that he just swayed where he stood. His heart felt as blue as the child's fingernails and lips.

The toboggan glided away, slowly at first, then gained speed, and soon shot off down the slope. The pompon on the child's hat swung about on the back of his head like a crazy pendulum, but before long it was reduced to the size of a snowflake and the plum-coloured figure diminished in bulk at the same rate. Ludvik followed the progress of the boy on his toboggan, watching until all he could see was a dark speck very far away. He had the impression it was his own childhood rushing away, in a furious, tearing hurry, having stood there in front of him, calling him to account, a challenge he had failed.

He finally set off again, and had to walk fast, for to his annoyance this encounter had delayed him. It seemed above all to have strangely displaced him in time. He felt as if he were making his way in the margin of the present, or rather as if he were hobbling between two time zones operating at different speeds, a bit like when you are walking on a travelator and the handrail moves more slowly alongside you; your feet feel light, swift, while your hand resting on the handrail drags along limply, and your body then feels a vague sense of disequilibrium in the rhythm surrounding it, bearing it, animating it. And this impression lasted for the entire duration of his long journey by bus and train.

So, it had taken no more than a petulant child standing by the road like some bird of ill-omen suddenly to deprive him, rob him, of all the respite he had found in Vladimira's barrel, of the tenderness he had experienced in the little cabin boy's company, of the deep silence imparted by the snow. As for the story of fat Ludmilla, which came back into his mind two or three times in the course of that journey, it did not make him laugh at all any more, nor did it relieve him of his anxiety. The story had eventually lost all its quirkiness and drollness. It was really no match for the unease prompted by these importunate encounters with individuals who seemed each time to appear out of nowhere in order to hurl reproaches at him, or jeers, or vague and distressing innuendoes. But in the name of what, of whom, did all these raisers of disquiet speak? Some of them seemed casually, innocently, to have given voice to an idea, doubt or reflection passing through his mind at that very same moment; others, to have made themselves the untimely mouthpiece sometimes of his unconscious, sometimes of his conscience, and now of his childhood. And yet nothing of what they said was clearly expressed, nor, above all, was it very coherent. They said far too much, and at the same time much too little, and it was this that most irritated Ludvik. Besides, he thought it was his own fault for always allowing himself to be taken by surprise and nonplussed, for not being ready with an answer, being slow to react. He could only endure these assaults and then flounder in the toils of ill-defined uncertainty. And as this went on, he felt a gradual erosion of the sediment of boredom for so long settled inside him, a loosening of the vice of disenchantment, of lassitude, that gripped his heart, but all the same without regaining any energy, enthusiasm, or cheerfulness. He was simply, insidiously, little by little, stripped naked. His carapace fell apart, his indifference fissured, his last certitudes cracked, and an increasing emptiness opened up. A desert of snow, of dust, extended inside him, encircling his reason that was slowly drifting amid growing uncertainty. Reality appeared double, collapsed in on itself, and frontiers and landmarks vanished. He felt as if he were the victim of a strange inward transformation, a progressive derangement in his powers of perception. Having once ventured a little too far in the maze of insane love and known its eddies and turbulences, he was now wary of any realm of excess and disorder. What he was experiencing certainly had nothing to do with amorous passion, but the transformation that was beginning to take place inside him nonetheless shared some disturbing similarities with that chaos of emotions, that destructive fervour, that jubilant disquiet. He no more wanted to head for the high seas of extreme love again, than to plumb his inner depths. He kept himself aloof as much from himself as from others.

It was not until he was at home again, back in his familiar setting, that Ludvik realized he had been neglecting Brum and Eva. He had actually thought of Brum during the first few days of his stay in the mountains, but each time those thoughts mingled, then blended, in a slow melting continuum, with his semi-grey, semi-pallid vision of the Magi, which in turn dissolved into the snow. But he had neither telephoned nor written. As it was very late, he put off till the next day acting on his decision to call Eva.

The next morning he went out to run a few errands. On his way back, he opened his letterbox; all he found inside was one envelope and three publicity leaflets. On his return the previous evening he had removed a good dozen letters and a whole heap of junk mail. He was going to slip this latest letter into his pocket to add it to the pile of correspondence he had not yet had time to go through properly, when he noticed the postmark on the envelope. It was stamped at the post office in T. So he did not wait until he was inside the apartment to open it; he tucked the bottle of milk and bag full of rolls he had just bought under his arm, and tore open the envelope as he climbed the stairs. It contained a simple card on which Eva had inscribed a few lines in her fine, very upright handwriting. 'Joachym died on Sunday, 23rd February, in the early evening. The date of the funeral has not yet been fixed.'

Ludvik's vision blurred and he did not read the next couple of lines. So Brum had died two days ago, while Ludvik was chatting with Vladimira. And suddenly a brief flash of illumination came into his mind: that famous Sunday, 10th Adar 5352, on which, according to one contemporary chronicler, the meeting between the Emperor Rudolph and the Maharal of Prague had taken place, was equivalent to 23rd February 1592 in the Christian calendar, in other words, exactly four hundred years before this recent Sunday, 23rd February 1992. It had taken the shock of receiving news of Brum's death for Ludvik finally to establish the correlation. This coincidence, which in any case may have been completely fortuitous and insignificant, at the time disconcerted Ludvik sufficiently to cause him a slight start of surprise. The bottle of milk slipped and broke on the steps. Ludvik hurried away to fetch a dustpan brush and a floorcloth. As he was picking up the bits of glass and mopping up the puddle of milk he reflected on this temporal game of mirrors that soon came to appear senseless. After all, of what concern was this event to Brum? Why should he have chosen to die on this particular date, which in any case was uncertain since another chronicler had set it a week earlier. And even if it were correct, was it enough to breath one's last on an important anniversary in order to obtain visiting rights to this precisely targeted past, and retrospective revelation of a secret that had remained impenetrable for centuries? Ludvik deemed this hypothesis absurd, it would never have occurred to him if Eva had not let drop so many obscure hints over the past few months.

He called Eva at once, but she was not at home; the haunting, isolated little notes of the ringing phone fell on emptiness. So he settled down at his desk, sorted through his mail, replied to a few letters, then corrected the proofs of two articles he had recently written, and finally reimmersed himself in his translation. Now he wanted to be finished as quickly as possible with this work that seemed always about to be completed and at the same time kept fraying like a badly-sewn hem. He considered he had devoted quite enough time to this difficult text for which he would not even be paid, and that no one would read, apart from his penniless publisher.

Seated in front of his computer, Ludvik found it harder and harder to concentrate. He blinked and rubbed his eyelids. He had in fact noticed that his eyesight had been weakening for some time, but this deterioration suddenly seemed to be going into free-fall. He telephoned several ophthalmologists and managed to arrange an appointment with one for the following morning. Finding himself debilitated, afflicted in his capacity to see, to read, Ludvik felt an anxiety that put all his other worries into the shade. In any case, those worries were imprecise, resulting from a conjunction of minor incidents, unsettling encounters, doubts and dissatisfactions, a sense of entrapment in what had become far too lonely a life. Whereas, here, he was dealing with a concrete problem, a physical failing, and not a mental perturbation. In fact, Ludvik was much more affected by all these events than he wanted to admit, and the deficiency of his eyesight served to channel his anxiety.

He did not manage to reach Eva until late afternoon. Her voice on the phone sounded deeper than usual to Ludvik, as if she were delivering her words into empty space. He dared not question her as to what significance she attributed to the day 'chosen' by her uncle for his death. He contented himself with asking for information of a much more practical nature. She told him that the date of the cremation had just been fixed; the ceremony was to take place the following week. Ludvik said he would like to come to T for that occasion. 'Very well,' Eva replied, in such a detached tone of voice that Ludvik felt rather offended, even annoyed. Yet he was accustomed to Eva's coldness.

The next day he went for his consultation. The letters danced at the end of the pointer the ophthalmologist moved about the chart. Screwing up his eyes and straining his neck, Ludvik said to himself,

'My eyesight's withering like Esther's bouquets of dried roses.' Then, while the eye-doctor made him go through some tedious eye exercises, a panic question chilled his heart: would he still recognize Esther if he walked past her in the street? And at that same moment Esther's face presented itself to him in a vision of painful clarity.

The doctor reassured him about the state of his eyesight, gave him a brief explanation about the lens' loss of elasticity and its reduced powers of accommodation, then made a few comments about the ill-effects of aging, and finally gave him a prescription for a pair of glasses.

As soon as he came out of the hospital, Ludvik went into an optician's, who promised that the glasses would be ready by the beginning of the week. Relieved to have managed to deal with this problem rapidly, Ludvik felt a desire to linger in town. It was cold but dry, the light was clear, and time had come back into alignment. Ludvik finally felt as if he were walking down the dead centre of the present again, and no longer hobbling in the margin of it. But this calm did not last long, it was suddenly shattered as he turned into a street. The street was deserted, and completely unexceptional, but someone, somewhere, was playing a clarinet, and Ludvik needed to hear only four or five notes to lose his placid composure in an instant.

The tune was familiar to him, very strangely familiar. Yet he did not know where or when he had heard it before. And the tune was repeated, once, twice, three times . . . It was a very short piece, full of liveliness, and as insistent as it was haunting. Ludvik stopped and retraced his footsteps a little way, until he found where the tune was coming from. A student harpsichordist in a music school room was practising this piece, with its jostling notes, trying to master the rhythm. Ludvik stood on the pavement and listened. The student sometimes broke off after a few bars and started again from the beginning, concentrating on a single phrase, under instructions from a teacher whose voice Ludvik could hear indistinctly whenever she raised it.

The tune skipped along, as brisk and bracing as a hail shower, fell silent for a moment only the more energetically to burst forth again; the notes struck the classroom windowpanes and their echo filled the street, hammering at Ludvik's temples. And he kept trying to recall where and when he had heard this tune, and above all why it so intrigued him, throwing him into an increasing state of tension, as if the student, by striking the keys of the harpsichord, were playing not on the strings but on his nerves. He discovered himself to be suffering an attack of paramnesia, a condition he had never suffered from before. His memory was thrown into alarm, his senses were all topsy-turvy, he was on tenterhooks with curiosity, and everything inside him quivered with futile overexcitement. The feeling that this was something he had heard before became so intense it was almost painful.

At last the lesson came to an end and the music stopped. But the tune continued to innervate Ludvik's body with a whole network of acidulous fibres that vibrated and tingled. He remained rooted to the spot, striving to contain and subdue the violent tumult of his wits. A little girl of about twelve came running up and rushed into the school lobby. He just had time to notice the red-blonde flash of her braided hair. A few seconds later she came out again, but in duplicate. She was flanked by a little girl in every respect identical to her, dressed in the same spinach-coloured coat and with the same hairstyle. However, a single detail differentiated them: the double was carrying a satchel in her right hand. Maybe this was the pupil who had just been practising that piece on the harpsichord over and over again. Ludvik went up to the twins and asked them. They stopped in front of him, holding hands, and fixed a distrustful gaze on him. Their temples and brows were fringed with little orange-coloured curls, as fine as copper shavings. As they remained on their guard, Ludvik repeated his question about the harpsichord tune he had heard as he passed by, and he said that he found it very beautiful and he would like to know the composer and the title of it. This explanation seemed to reassure the little girls, and the one with the satchel said a few words that Ludvik did not understand, so she repeated them, trying hard to articulate every syllable distinctly, just as she had had to keep her finger movements well defined just now in order to strike each string of the instrument accurately, to give the sound all its clarity. But her pronunciation, proving no more successful than her playing, which had not really satisfied her teacher, failed to convey what Ludvik wanted to know. The little girl displayed a certain annoyance, and with a peevish shrug, as if to say, 'These adults are such bores! They're never happy, and besides they never cotton on to anything!', she opened her satchel, took out a musical score which she waved under Ludvik's nose. He read: 'My Lady Carey's Dompe – Anonymous.'

The pretty redhead chirped, 'There, that's it, and it's jolly difficult, I can tell you!' Then she thrust her score back inside her school-bag, banged the recalcitrant fastener lightly with her fist, took hold of her sister's hand again, and they both went off, with their braids swinging.

'My Lady Carey's Dompe'. This title did not enlighten Ludvik at all, and the anonymity of the composer only made more annoying the anonymity of this curious recollection, or rather sense of recollection that the music had summoned up in him. He in turn wandered off, lost in thought: he went on searching his memory until that evening, trying to identify in what place and on what day he must have heard that tune, but without success. Yet an image stole into mind two or three times in the course of his inward investigation, that of the frog-headed statues of the Latone fountain. But he was incapable of establishing a link between the park at Versailles and 'My Lady Carey's Dompe'. So once again he admitted defeat, and gave up his search, just as he had given up trying to throw light on the areas of obscurity sown by the various nutcases he had had the misfortune to encounter in recent months.

*

Towards the end of the week he visited the editorial offices of the magazine for which he worked, and those of the two newspapers for which he occasionally wrote articles. He felt the need to renew his contact with people, to communicate with them other than by telephone or by mail. He needed to regain his foothold in reality. It was no use minimizing, and even contriving to ignore, the incidents that had occurred over the past few months, he could not rid himself of a certain unease. A breach had opened up inside him, he was no longer truly certain of anything. He was even reduced sometimes to doubting his own presence in the density and roughness of the world, of which he had now and then such a fanciful perception, as though distorted, or out of kilter. Having others listen directly to what he said both alarmed and reassured him; while talking, he would watch the expression and reaction of those he was speaking to, to try and work out whether they suspected him of madness, or at least detected some oddity in him. But they were all far too preoccupied with their own affairs to take that much notice of him.

He also went by the office of his bankrupt publisher, Adam. He found him more disillusioned than ever, but calm and stolid on the raft of his disenchantment. Ludvik mentioned the news of Brum's death.

'I never met him,' said Adam, 'but I've often heard people speak of him, always to his credit. I read some of the translations he did, poems by Heine, Hofmannsthal, Mörike, Trakl . . . he was a remarkable translator. I was told that he lived a very secluded life, even a little unsociable, somewhere in the provinces.'

'In T,' said Ludvik. 'After he was forced out of the university, he went and settled there with his niece, who became more of an adopted daughter to him. They lived alone together, surrounded by books and silence.'

'You couldn't wish for better company,' remarked Adam. 'Did you know him well?'

'In the past, yes, I was his student. His lectures were magnificent, he always seemed to talk off the cuff, to let himself be carried along by the inspiration of words, he was constantly drawing on the undercurrent of the countless poems he knew by heart. His whole being hummed with this quintessential murmur. I remained close to him for many years. Then our relationship became less close, and afterwards I left the country.'

'What kind of man was he?'

'I told you, a dreamer of words, a speaking anthology. But outside his lectures, he didn't say much, he was very reserved. A loner full of melancholy courtesy. But when I saw him again last October, he was already no more than a shadow of himself, a worn-out old man burping incoherent noises.'

'Oh, death rarely bothers with niceties, even with the most delightfully courteous of people. It arrives unpredictably, cutting you short without regard for time or place, still less for any decorum.'

'It's true that the end of Brum's life was particularly drawn-out and upsetting, but it may be that his death was only so long in coming because he, Brum, delayed it so fiercely . . .'

'It's not enough to have devoted your whole life to meditating, dreaming on the words of poets, to be spared the anguish of dying. Death may be a word on which you can endlessly expand or even poetize all your life, but it's certainly no longer a fine subject for reverie when that transition occurs, when it crudely imposes itself as the negation of reality. There are great saints who have screamed with terror at the moment of death, so why not your Brum . . .'

'No,' protested Ludvik, who suddenly allowed himself to get caught up in considerations that, after all, he had so far taken care to avoid. 'In Brum's case, it's a different matter. It's not fear that kept him alive, on the contrary . . . a strange curiosity needled him.'

'What do you mean?'

'It would appear that he chose the date of his death, and he only battled so hard to reach the day that he had determined on.'

'A reprieve such as a translator, who hasn't finished a piece of work on time, might wrest for himself?' said Adam ironically. 'And was he successful?'

'Yeah,' said Ludvik, with a wry smile, 'except that death never goes bankrupt.'

'Don't take it badly,' said Adam, getting up to go and fetch a bottle and two glasses, which he set down on his desk. 'Here, let's drink to our health as bankrupt survivors.'

Ludvik drained his glass, then held it out for a refill, declaring, 'And now, to Brum's memory!'

'To Brum,' Adam concurred, pouring a second round of adulterated brandy. 'So, let's get back to your complicated story about the date of his death . . .'

But Ludvik regained control of himself, he did not want to raise this problem. He remained intrigued, of course, by the supposed mystery of Brum's death, but he was loathe to reveal his doubts on the matter. He was evasive.

'Oh, nothing serious! In fact, just some complicated speculations on the part of his niece. Grief sometimes prompts people to come up with some funny ideas, some crazy notions, in their confusion . . . Let's leave old Brum in peace now, and talk about something else.'

Adam nevertheless gave him a searching look, half-ironic, half-suspicious, then declared, 'Very well, let's not pursue it. So tell me about the text for which I granted you "such a generous" reprieve . . . Is the translation nearing completion, or have you given up on it?'

'I haven't given up, I've nearly finished. There are just a few details left to deal with. The final touches.'

'I'm looking forward to reading it, and I hope it won't lie mouldering in a drawer for too long. I'm soon going to be emptying my drawers, but I'll do my utmost to make sure that a text such as the one you've been translating doesn't fall into oblivion, and gets taken up by another publisher. I've already told you, it's surprisingly modern. The Maharal offers a very acute, very profound analysis of the contradiction that is tearing the world apart internally, and of the essential contrariness that torments the soul of man, and his vision of the void separating God and man is of immense subtlety.'

'You seem to be very well acquainted with his thinking, I doubt that the book I've been translating will contain anything new to you.'

'You're wrong,' said Adam, 'my knowledge of his work is very superficial, but the little that I know makes me want to learn more, and I'm curious about any commentary on his work, or even any reference to it.'

'I didn't know you were so interested in theological issues,' remarked Ludvik.

'Convinced atheists are just as rare as believers with unquestioning confidence in their faith. Let's say that I belong to that indeterminate race of tormented unbelievers that exist just as much as doubting believers. And what about you, which side are you on?'

'I'm afraid I'm very much on my own. I don't care one way or the other,' confessed Ludvik.

'A pity, that's how you end up losing sight of yourself.'

This comment by Adam disturbed Ludvik. For a moment he pictured the little boy throwing salt on the snow. And he heard the voice of the child who shouted at him, choking with rage, 'You've forgotten everything! You've let the savour of everything fade . . .' He closed his eyes to dispel the image of the little bird-catcher with a gaze that was the dark blue of a stormy sky, with purple lips and fingernails.

'Is something wrong?' asked Adam.

'No, it's nothing. My eyes have been playing me up for a while. I occasionally get slight blackouts. I'll be getting a pair of glasses soon.'

Ludvik got up to leave. Adam accompanied him to the door.

'I hope you'll be back before long, with your translation under your arm, and with your new pair of glasses on!'

'By the way,' said Ludvik, suddenly curious about something he had never thought of before, 'how did you come to find out about this book that you asked me to translate?'

His publisher gave an amused smile. 'It should hardly come as any surprise to you: it was through reading an article by your dear Brum that appeared in a samizdat publication shortly before the regime changed, in which he mentioned this work, and praised it.'

'An article by Brum?'

'Yes, indeed, but enough of that. Didn't you say just now that we'd better leave old Brum in peace? Well, good-bye.'

And Adam gently closed the door.

Ludvik hesitated for a moment on the landing, then decided to overlook this – after all, trifling – little treachery of Adam's, and he descended the stairs. What did it matter, in the end, whether Adam found out about this text through Brum? There wasn't even anything suprising in the fact that Brum, being the great explorer of books that he was, should have discovered this text and been interested by it. This did not in itself confirm any suspicions of some mysterious relationship between Brum's death and a key episode in the life of the Maharal of Prague. However, to cut short any incipient revival of his misgivings, Ludvik decided to go to a billiard hall, to give himself something else to think about.

The next day he devoted his morning to tidying up and housework. While dusting the shelves of his bookcase, he knocked to the ground the milky-toned, sand-coloured greetings card. Its corners were a bit bent and the paper was beginning to warp slightly. Ludvik put the card on his desk. To flatten it out, he placed a big transparent, slightly iridescent, glass ball on it, containing a few various-sized bubbles of air, which he used as a paperweight. Standing on the back of the card, this glass paperweight fulfilled a different function, that of a magnifying glass, but a slighty crazed, distorting magnifying glass. The words written in sepia ink seemed to have exploded and the colour of the ink was edged with shades of red, orange, yellow, and ringed with purple. Ludvik poured over this magnifying glass and took pleasure in watching the letters undulate and become distorted at the least movement of his head, like slender dark-ochre algae at the bottom of an aquarium. A few words took shape for a moment before curving, spreading out, breaking formation. He caught two words – 'risk' and 'opportunity'. So he slid the glass ball very slowly over the lines, in order to read the scrawl he had so far neglected to decipher. The Christmas card finally yielded its indistinct message amid the bubbles of air locked inside the magnifying glass.

'They have been travelling for so long. If we delay too much, we risk losing sight of them. Yet their wandering is our opportunity. It is time we set out. All my best wishes for a safe journey. Adieu. Yours Joachym Brum.'

Ludvik felt his blood abruptly drain away, then flood through him again with feverish heat. He shut his eyes for a moment. Old Brum's face of suffering, his bewildered gaze, appeared before him, as clear beneath his closed eyelids as if the aged man were right in front of him. He finally appreciated how grave, inexcusable, his negligence towards Brum had been. Not content with having let a growing remoteness establish itself between them in the past, then having shown scant concern for Brum during his own years of exile, Ludvik had only paid him one visit since his return. And his careless disregard had continued: he lost the notebook Eva gave him, without even having had the curiosity to glance at it; he made no attempt to find it; all that time it took the old man to die, he never really insisted on returning to T; and finally he did not even work out that the author of the illegible greetings card was Brum – could only be Brum. Yet all he had to do was check the postmark on the back of the card and he would have been put on the right track immediately.

With his memory failing, his language skills

deserting him, his life disintegrating, Brum had nevertheless managed to tear himself from death's embrace to set down in handwriting as tremulous as his voice these few epiphanic lines on the back of a card the colour of milk, of sand, of tears and ashes. The colour of his embattled heart, ready for departure. The effort it must have cost him to write these strange, final greetings, must surely have been huge and exhausting. But he, Ludvik, had not deigned to linger more than a few minutes over this card, in fact he had almost thrown it away.

He pored over the card once more, and inspected the other side of it this time. He proceeded in the same way as when deciphering the lines, sliding the spherical magnifying glass across it. The grain of the image and the subtleties of the colour tones appeared more distinctly. He thought he could distinguish three ghostly figures, wan shadows reduced to powder on pale sand, or yellow snow. But this scrutiny eventually made his eyes hurt. He closed his eyelids and pressed his fingers to them. Then in the darkness of his body two dark blue smudges appeared: the gaze at once harsh and imploring of the little salt-scatterer. And again he felt himself turn blue, right through to his heart. He opened his eyes and collapsed onto a chair, but the child's gaze continued to fix him inwardly, intensely, with pain, with violence. Ludvik felt profoundly confused. Different memories, sensations and feelings mingled inside him. He wished he could console this child, do the right thing by him, and at the same time drive him from his thoughts for ever. He could see faces that surfaced within him, overlaying each other, blending into each other: little Lubosek's face turned into that of the bird-catcher; the bird-catcher's lengthened until it looked like that of the young man with the salt rose who, in turn, was transfigured, assuming the features of the old newspaper vendor, which faded to give way to Brum's face . . . this series of transformations was endless. All these faces melting into one another gave rise to a silent drama, a strange visual drama in which Ludvik discovered himself to be absent, and at the same time summoned to appear.

A sudden noise startled him. A squall of melted snow gusted through the yard, moaning, shaking the bare trees and making the washing hung out on the balconies flap. Ludvik got up and looked out of the window. The familiar landscape enclosed in the yard acquired fantastic aspects: clouds of whirling snow suggestive of draped human figures driven before the wind, and white sheets and cloths like shrouds after the resurrection. But in the same instant the squall carried its busy tidying over the rooftops, and Ludvik decided to call it a day. Besides he was short of household cleaning materials and so he found a very good reason to go out for a walk, with the excuse of having some shopping to do.

With a basket over his arm, and with his back bowed, taking small steps, he walked along the supermarket aisles displaying domestic products. The reason he was examining the shelves so closely was because he had an annoying tendency to confuse items, especially in aerosol cans. He had already put a tin of scouring powder in his basket, a pack of sponges for washing dishes, a bottle of lavatory cleaner and disinfectant, a long-stemmed feather duster of a fluorescent apple-green with garish pink feathers, when he bumped into another shopper. They both dropped their baskets, whose contents rolled on to the ground. Ludvik and the other shopper crouched down to pick up their purchases, and it was then that they recognized each other. He found himself face to face, and knee to knee, with Katia.

'Well I never,' she exclaimed, 'the elusive Ludvik! This is an awful surprise, isn't it? So, the confirmed old bachelor with the untamed heart is out doing his little errands?'

'Listen to the wild cat talking!' replied Ludvik, hastily throwing the items into his basket. 'Besides, aren't you the single housewife doing the same little errands? Here, this oven cleaner and this lovely metal scourer belong to you. Each to his own.'

They stood up, staring at each other, like stuck pigs. Suddenly Katia burst out laughing.

'What are you doing with a feather duster the colour of a pig's snout? You bring all the elegance of a maid in a bordello to keeping your house clean!'

Ludvik took a sidelong glance at his duster and laughed too.

'All right! Shall we proceed to the checkout and then go and get ourselves a drink somewhere?' suggested Katia.

They went into a wine bar with dark wooden tables and chairs. They sat at a table at the back of the room, and ordered a bottle of tokay. Once she had got over her initial bad-temperedness, Katia appeared calm. She did not bear any grudge against Ludvik for the inconsiderate way in which he behaved towards her.

‘Yes,’ she said, ‘in the end, I don’t mind, because you’re not really important to me. Right from the start, from when we first met, we knew it wasn’t a matter of love between us. Because you and I once had our hearts so badly broken, we’re no longer capable of being swept off our feet, of falling in love again. We take what’s offered, or allow ourselves to be taken, but our hearts are shrivelled, like that dried-out orange peel I found round my wrist, the morning I woke up in my bed that you’d just deserted without further ceremony. That was a fine non-love poem you composed there, a charming declaration of a heart’s incapacity.’

‘And yet,’ said Ludvik, ‘apparently in olden days, in China, young girls were offered oranges by men who wished to marry them. I didn’t pick the right fruit for taking my leave.’

‘On the contrary, yes, you did, since you left only the skin, not the fruit in all its ripeness. Anyway, let’s not talk about it any more, it’s all in the past now, and it’s best left that way. Let’s be content to drink a toast now and again. To the memory of our love grown cold, and to the health of passing time.’

Ludvik remained silent, with an absent look in his eyes. He thought he could hear welling up, deep inside him, a mournful surge of grey water.

'You look very morose,' said Katia. 'If I've stirred gloomy thoughts in your mind, you can brush them away with your fuchsia feather duster.'

'No, I just feel, how can I put it? A slight emptiness . . .'

'Emptiness? Oh, yes,' said Katia. 'From now on, the feeling's one of emptiness, slight, great, or terrible. But maybe this phase of emptiness is a salutary experience? A kind of ordeal even? When love goes, when your beloved snatches it away from you and takes everything else along with it, you suddenly find yourself completely naked, and you confront yourself in a new light, a brutal, scouring light, and you get to know yourself in the raw. Masks off!'

'And beneath the mask, what have you discovered?'

'That's what I continue to ask myself. It's me, without being me, a different me, one purged of the passionate woman-in-love who for so long reigned supreme, dictating her law and her extravagances. She's a very ordinary woman, like a flea perched on the vastness of time, jogging along her way amid general indifference.'

'Is it really necessary to be ditched in order to gauge your own limitations and your own banality?'

'Of course not, but it helps. Passion is so turbulent, so noisy, monopolizing and exclusive, for as long as it holds sway over us – even in the pain of being abandoned, indeed especially then – that it has a tendency to blinker us, to make us unmindful of everything that doesn't in one way or another flatter our obsession. I've finally reached the stage of total contentment, of calm; that's to say, I've stopped wanting to run away from the emptiness that has opened up inside me, I've even learned how to remain standing, I've conquered my vertigo. And there, in that austere desert of heart and mind, I'm discovering a strange intensity of being. Sometimes I sense the promise of some great beauty, of a gentle dazzlement . . . I don't know how to explain it . . . What I do know, at least what I feel, is that everything remains to be accomplished . . .'

'What do you mean by everything?'

'It's difficult to pin down. It seems like nothing, undefined, limitless. I strive to quieten within me protracted old murmurings, in order to catch the very faintest resonances that penetrate the silence. Perhaps everything that remains to be accomplished is just that: learning to wonder at little things, to lend an ear to sighs that have risen from the horizon very unobtrusively, to wander endlessly within the four walls of your room. Then to find yourself where you weren't expecting to be and to be, other than you had imagined yourself. To sense within you the rustling and quivering of time passing, life quietly at work within your blood, to renew your vision of the world and of others, unassumingly but thoroughly.'

Katia drank a sip of wine, put down her glass again, then added after a moment's silence, 'And I've no wish, none at all, to be caught up again in the turmoils of passion, with all its latent volcanoes. I've learned to love differently. With detachment. I want to keep my hands not only free but also, and above all, empty. Ever more empty.'

'That sounds a bit like indifference, or at least a germ of it. Don't you think?' asked Ludvik.

'Is that something you'd know about?' said Katia.

'Yes, I'm afraid so. And yet . . .'

'Well, go on . . . finish the sentence. Yet what?'

'I don't know. I'm increasingly losing the thread of myself, I sometimes feel as if I'm cracking up, like an old abandoned house.'

'Be careful, that's how ghosts get in and start squatting on the premises.'

'No need for ghosts. You only have to leave the house, pass someone in the street, exchange a few words with a stranger, for doubts, or unease, to insinuate themselves. For a while now, I've been finding that people are weird. At least, sometimes. But perhaps it's just that I'm no longer attuned.'

'Unless it's the opposite,' suggested Katia. 'It may very well be that on the contrary you're only just beginning to get attuned? People are always a bit weird, if we only observe them carefully. Everyone has their eccentricities, tics of gesture or expression, style of language, way of appropriating words and returning to some of them, always the same ones, constantly. Above all, everyone has a grain of madness, more or less developed, sown in some corner of their brain. We don't see the grain that's germinating in our own flesh, and creeping stealthily through our veins and nerves, like an invisible ivy, eventually developing into thickets in our hearts and minds, but we notice the grain sprouting in others. You're finally opening your eyes to others, that's all.'

'It's possible,' was all Ludvik said, already unwilling to pursue this discussion and raise certain issues that were troubling him. As soon as he was about to broach the subject, as with Adam the day before, he hesitated and almost immediately backtracked, for he did not know how to tackle it. He felt as if he were on moving sands, losing the thread before even managing to find it. But Katia, who had long been roaming the regions of mist, cold and torment essentially quite similar to those in which Ludvik was now lost, was vaguely aware of his confusion and so, prompted by some obscure impulse, she continued to develop the thoughts that were on her mind.

'It's good that people seem a bit weird to us, it's a sign at least that we've registered their presence, and that we've noticed something different in them. Sometimes this particularity isn't of much interest, and other times it is. What matters is that they should jolt us, surprise us, shake up our ideas. We ought never to be left unscathed, or least unchanged, by any encounter, whatever it might be. We should always undergo some change, even if only by an atom. There is an Hassidic legend that says every individual has a light in the sky that is theirs alone, and when two people meet, so too do their lights. And from this contact a new light is born, which is called an angel. But this angel born of the encounter of two living beings is ephemeral, its life span is twelve months, so it disappears if at the end of a year the two people responsible for its birth haven't seen each other again. Every angel born of an encounter dies after too long an absence. In order for it to shine, the two sources of its light need to remain in contact on earth.'

'Well,' exclaimed Ludvik, 'with all the breakdowns in emotional relationships of every kind that take place on earth, the sky must be littered with the remains of neglected angels!'

'Yes and no. Legend also has it that an angel that dies as a result of the separation of those who engendered it, can be reborn if those two people come together again, and pronounce a blessing when they greet each other. They must invoke He who restores the dead to life.'

She stopped talking, and they both stared at each other for a moment in silence, as the same thought crossed their minds, then they exchanged a rather sad smile.

'Hmm,' said Ludvik, pouring wine into both glasses, 'if by a miracle the angel of a certain relationship I once had, which shattered into a thousand very sharp-edged pieces, were to be restored to life, it wouldn't look too good. It would resemble Lazarus summoned from his tomb and already rotting away beneath his shroud. Anyway, let's drink to the health of our dear departed angels!'

'A descent into the grave or a spell in limbo must surely leave some mark, but why should those traces be only ugliness and rictuses? If by a miracle, as you say, the angel of a lost passion can come to life again, it must be reborn transfigured. Disfigured and grimacing angels are of absolutely no interest, they don't even make sense. The angel of reunion, whoever might be reunited, must be all luminous with forgiveness, indulgence, gentleness, otherwise there's no angel. So let's drink to the health of more unassuming angels than those catapulted by passion. To the angel of the present moment!'

As she raised her glass, half-filled with amber wine, she saw Ludvik through it. 'Your head's upside down, like a funny little bubble of sunshine. Is that a grape seed inside it or a seed of madness?'

At these words Ludvik thought of Brum's card, which he had read that same morning with the aid of an improvised and distorting magnifying glass, full of air bubbles, and the two words 'risk' and 'opportunity' appeared wavering before his eyes.

'So which is it?' asked Katia, still tilting her glass and eyeing him through it.

'You can't have one without the other,' replied Ludvik without thinking.

'That's true,' admitted Katia, finally deciding to raise her glass to her lips, 'everything comes with its opposite. Besides, it's all a question of perspective, of viewpoint and interpretation.'

When they left the café the sky was already turning a purplish brown. They parted in pouring rain.

'Foul weather for angels,' remarked Ludvik.

'Not to mention your feather duster,' said Katia, pointing at Ludvik's bag, with the pink feathers sticking out, all limp and pathetic.

Ludvik spent his Sunday finishing off the house-cleaning and tidying-up that he had only made a start on the day before. In the evening, when everything was finally in order, he contemplated the spick-and-span state of his apartment and, far from experiencing a little satisfaction, all he felt was overwhelming boredom. This precarious neatness, this ephemeral cleanliness, seemed to mock him, to underline the vanity of his existence devoted to small tasks endlessly to be carried out all over again and, to be put right. It reminded him of the lack of perseverance in his thinking that was never followed through, the woolliness of his doubts that came to nothing, and would gather dust again, from one day to the next. He felt so out of place in this well-ordered space that he quickly dressed to go out. Then, as ever when his mood blackened in this way, he headed for a billiard hall.

As he was circling round the table, observing the position of the balls and considering the best way to play his next move, an unbidden thought entered his mind, disturbing his concentration – that of the legend Katia had related to him about the angel born of every encounter. He bent right over the cloth, eyed up his ball, targeted his strike, estimated how hard to hit it, with all skillfulness, and played a superb stroke. As he rubbed the tip of his billiard cue with chalk, he wondered about the angel that might have resulted from the famous encounter between the Emperor Rudolph and the Maharal of Prague: an angel of intense brightness, certainly. But was it only a brief flash of light, just as long as the interview between the two men went on, dying out soon afterwards like a spectacular fire of straw, or had it lasted? Ludvik imagined it lying at the bottom of the Deer Pit, or else gliding across the white stones of the basilica of St George, like a powdery ray of sunshine. But no, history had so badly traduced it that it could not have survived. And yet, what if Brum had managed to rediscover its trace? But in what form, what place, and by what means? Nowhere other than in himself, and by means of suffering, of slow detachment and long patience, by means of exile from himself, until the ultimate escape of death. This conjecture, from the moment it was formulated, bothered him. It contained a contradiction, juxtaposing the deepest inwardness with total outwardness. He was still very diligently chalking the tip of his billiard cue without being aware of the absurdity of his gesture. Then he skipped over the apparent contradiction. He recalled what Katia had said, after having observed him through her glass of wine, that everything is a matter of perspective, of viewpoint and interpretation, an opinion also held by the Maharal. According to him everything can simultaneously exist in a certain way, and in another radically different way, depending on the angle from which it is considered: from the smallness of the finite or the expansiveness, the boundary-breaking reach of the infinite and of eternity; from a blinkered human perspective, often afflicted with shortsightedness, even close to blindness, or from a divine perspective of boundless radiance. There was disproportion, distortion and even conflict where these two ways of looking at the universe intersected – and above all a rift between the two visions of each other. It was this point of intersection that the Maharal had spent his whole life striving to reach. Had he discussed this with the Emperor Rudolph, during their secret meeting?

'Hey,' interjected an irritated voice that made Ludvik jump, 'I think your billiard tip's done, you've been chalking it for long enough! If you don't mind moving, I need a little space!' Two players were standing at the next table, and Ludvik, planted like a pillock between their table and his own, was in their way. He apologized and began to play again, but he was too distracted, and he pathetically missed all the shots he set up. He decided to stop, and left the hall, exasperated by the sneering laughter behind his back from the two players he had annoyed. Out in the street, he lit up a cigarette and then noticed that his fingers were all stained with blue chalk.

Two days later he went to the optician to pick up his glasses. When he settled them on his nose and looked at himself in the mirror, he felt uncomfortable, the arms squeezed his temples, the lenses blurred his vision even more, and he did not like the metal frames. He hastily put them away in their case, which he slipped into his pocket. He went into a beer hall. As he drained his tankard, he fiddled with the case inside his pocket, but dared not take it out, as if it were something shameful or ridiculous. He waited until he was in a somewhat deserted street before trying on his glasses again, and he walked for a while with the spectacles perched on his nose, stopping in front of signs and posters to test his vision. The sense of slight vertigo persisted, even if his eyes were already beginning to get used to the lenses and perceived more clearly the visible, and especially the legible, world around him. He wandered the streets like this for quite a long time, in order to put to the test what he called his new eyes, and he wavered between satisfaction and annoyance. He could see more distinctly, admittedly, but everything was slightly swimming around him. He looked at his watch. He still had time to go by the hospital and maybe he would get the chance of a quick consultation with the ophthalmologist.

He sat waiting on a bench in a long corridor. A door opened, a guy came out, with a fresh new bandage over one eye, and immediately the woman also waiting not far away from him got up, with her little squint-eyed son at her side, and disappeared into the consulting room. Ludvik found himself alone in the corridor. A woman in a grubby overall appeared at the end of the corridor. She was carrying a bucket and broom. She began to clean the linoleum; it was the colour of coffee made with curdled milk. When she got to where Ludvik was sitting, she set down her bucket, in which she soaked her floorcloth before energetically wringing it; her bared forearms had a sinuous quality and looked like supple roots of milky white. Ludvik glanced at her face, over the rim of his glasses. She had hollow cheeks and a wide dark-red mouth, her black eyes were ringed with a light brownish-yellow, and her already greying chestnut hair was tied back at the nape of her neck with a strip of gauze. He admired her very white slender neck, the solemnity of her features, and found her austerely beautiful.

At that point he removed his glasses and rubbed the bridge of his nose. The woman blurred. So he had to stare at her rather desperately when she said to him, 'You'll have to get used to seeing the world through those specs of yours, it's what comes of growing old.'

She had a deep, slightly rough voice that Ludvik liked, so he preferred to laugh at her impertinence, and replied with a smile, 'It's all right for you, you don't have to wear them.'

She corkscrewed her cloth on the end of her broom and resumed her task, then said in that husky voice, 'I look at the world with my heart bared, I see the hardships of the humblest folk magnified, and the magnificence of the powerful diminished. Nothing can make my vision normal.'

She pushed her bucket on with one foot and continued cleaning a little further ahead. Intrigued by this remark and fascinated by the rather harsh timbre of her voice, Ludvik turned in her direction and asked her what she meant by that. The woman did not reply until a few seconds later, with her back to him.

'What I said is simple enough, so why do you need any further explanation?' And she fell silent again, washing the floor all the while.

Ludvik in fact had no need at all for any explanation, he just wanted to hear the beautiful sound of her voice. He watched her as she worked. Her legs were as thin and delicately muscled as her arms, she wore old shapeless espadrilles and grey wool socks that bagged round her ankles, revealing very pronounced tendons and a little of the roundness of her heels. He wanted to keep the conversation going, so lacking inspiration, he reeled off a few platitudes to get her talking again.

'Of course, in your job, you come into contact with patients every day . . .'

She turned abruptly towards him. 'What do you know about my job?'

Taken aback by this rudeness, and especially by the ink-black gaze that she fixed on him, he could only stammer, 'Well . . . you're responsible for keeping the premises clean, here in this hospital, and that . . .'

'That what? Why not come straight to the point? You're not going to give me a lecture like some medical chief addressing the lower orders, are you? I'm the char on duty, that's all. I say it without apology or defiance. I speak plainly.' She resumed her task.

Ludvig dared not persist with this conversation, which was turning sour far too quickly, never mind about the underlying melody of her voice. He immediately put his glasses back on. But the woman soon started talking again, as she squatted by her bucket and thrust her floorcloth in it once more.

'Washing is a great thing, you know. When you wash the floor, you wipe away the traces left by the soles of dirty shoes, but not the footprints, you can never wipe away the footprints, they resonate in your heart for ever. And washing blood from wounds leaves your palms and your dreams stained red for ever. And washing the dead puts a lustre on their skin, but there's still a breath emanating from every pore. It's the departing soul, all amazed to be relieved of its flesh, to be suddenly so naked. You feel this breath brushing your hand, seeking to rest on the tips of your fingernails. After washing the dead, you're left for ever with a silence in your heart. It's the same ordeal as Maundy Thursday, every time; the tabernacle's empty. God is elsewhere, always and so strangely, terribly, elsewhere. That's what a corpse is, an empty tabernacle, from which the spirit of the living has gone. And no one really knows where.'

She got her cloth ready to use again, after squeezing it out, with brown water dripping from it.

'And tears, sir, washing away tears! I'm not just talking about those exuding inside the flesh, quietly trickling in the throat, from the neck to the kidneys, and mingling with the blood, breath, saliva, and sweat. The number of people with long stalactites of salt tears in the pit of their guts! When you wash the sick on the wards you hear the seeping of these invisible stalactites, and when you wash the dead you hear the disintegrating of these concretions of tears.'

Ludvik listened, heedless of the time, or even of his glasses perched crookedly on his nose. He observed the woman going up and down the corridor, bent over her broom, and who punctuated her soliloquy with unpredictable silences. Her voice moved away and drew closer, as she came and went.

'Ah, and the tears of women!' she said, tossing back a lock of her untidy hair. 'There's a proverb that dares to say, morning rain dries as quickly as women's tears, a pretty dew of no great substance. But what do men know about it? What do they, who won't allow themselves to cry, actually know of our sorrows, fears and anguish? Nothing! And what do we know of one another's hidden tears? Nothing! And of the tears of the angels hobbling in the shadows of us heedless sinners? Less than nothing! As for the tears that God sheds in the secret depths of his solitude, we're completely ignorant of them. At best we call them silence, at worst we talk of culpable silence.'

She hunkered down again, scrubbed at a stain, then stood up, threw the cloth into the bucket, which she lifted by the handle, grabbed the broom in the other hand, and came back towards Ludvik. Then her voice assumed even slower and deeper inflections.

'All these tears, sir, that form stalactites in the pit of our guts, spiral round our hearts, imbue our dreams and memories, and disintegrate on the day we die, well, they exude the salt of oblation. For, like it or not, dying is an oblation. Made to non-existence, or to God? You have to bet on it, heads or tails, there's no middle way, no easy way out. It's all or nothing. You have to bet, you have to take your chance.'

She stopped for a moment, rested the broom against her shoulder and with one hand wound the rebellious lock of hair behind her ear again. Her hands were reddened, chapped, and her nails were pared. The more Ludvik heard and saw of her, the more surprised he was by the contrasts in her. The language she used was disconcerting, apparently so little in accord with the job she did, and similarly her slender appearance, her solemn proud beauty, were at odds with her dirty overall, her shapeless socks, the wretched strip of gauze tying back her hair. And above all, her words contained obscure resonances that threw Ludvik's mind into alarm more than ever before. But he dared not say anything, or ask any questions. A great coldness spread through him.

The woman took hold of her broom, and set off again. She passed in front of Ludvik, but paid no attention to him, as if he were not there, and she continued her monologue.

'Maybe at the hour of our death it's the weight of the salt left by our tears that tips the departing soul in the right direction, where God remains silent. Yes, tips it in the direction of the vast and the luminous, even if you betted against it. The salt of tears is so heavy, it burns for such a long time, it could very well tip everything, set everything ablaze, purify everything, even at the very last minute. How are we to know? Is it not written: "And every oblation of thy meal offering shalt thou season with salt; neither shalt thou suffer the salt of the covenant of thy God to be lacking from thy meal offering: with all thine oblations thous shalt offer salt"? Since death is an oblation, well, what other salt should we add, if not the salt of our tears? Salt to purify, but even more important, much more important, to increase thirst. For which has the greater thirst of the other, man or God, and above all which of them has the greater need that the other should have thirst of him? How can we tell! With love, you can never tell. Did not Christ on the cross, at the moment of dying, say, "I thirst"? The reason being, that he had drunk all the tears of men, and also tasted those of God. He died at the confluence of these tears, at the meeting of these two thirsts.'

And with these words delivered to the rhythm of her majestic slow pace, with her bucket swinging like a metronome, and the broom she pushed in front of her like a salt-maker with his rake, the woman disappeared through a door at the end of the corridor. Ludvik felt his heart thumping and his temples clamped in an icy grip. His glasses were no longer the problem, in fact they slipped off his nose and fell to the ground. One lens dropped out and the other cracked. There was no point in waiting in this corridor any more. He picked up the lens and the frame, and he too left. He did not even make any attempt to find the charlady after her unsettling monologue. What purpose would that have served? If he had tried to asked her any questions, she would surely have retorted once again, 'What I said is simple enough, so why do you need any further explanation?'

When he got back home, he was astonished by the neatness of the place. He stood on the threshold of his study for a moment, contemplating the tidied shelves. He heard the muffled striking of the neighbours' clock on the other side of the wall, seven pretty chimes. Ludvik stared at this familiar space, listening to the sounds from within the building and those that came from the street. Life was following its course, slowly, quite normally, peacefully. He registered this, he felt himself to be perfectly calm and lucid, and at the same time an undercurrent was dragging his life elsewhere. The slow infiltration of the unusual into the texture of his everyday life, over the weeks and months, had now turned into a tide of strangeness that in a seemingly harmless manner was submerging the whole of the real world. And he was doubtful of everything, with an acute, indeterminate doubt, and prepared for anything. He had the impression there was no longer any refuge, anywhere, where he could regain his foothold in the simplicity of the real world. He did not attempt to track down the source of this tide of unreality that mingled with the otherwise unexceptional course of his life. In any case, he would have been unable to say whether it was a flood of the unreal, or the surreal, or even the para-real, or the infra-real. He had no word to define the ever-growing unease inside him, he felt only a very strong sense of being inwardly overwhelmed, of his consciousness dividing. He no longer had the strength, nor the desire, to fight against the flow of this incomprehensible current, for perhaps it had only gathered and swelled like this because he had tried to resist it, to escape? So if he let himself be overtaken and carried along by it, like a shipwrecked castaway floating on his back to save his energy, maybe this tide would exhaust itself?

The next morning he caught the train early. He was travelling to T. The ceremony was scheduled for late morning. He would go straight from the station to the cemetery, then he would catch a train back mid-afternoon or early evening, depending on what happened during the day. He hoped that Eva would invite him home with her for a while, he wanted one last chance to see the apartment in Linden Street where Brum had spent his old age. He recalled the amber light in the living-room, the big bookcases covering the walls, the strong smell of wax from the furniture and the wooden floor, the old, mostly dark-wine-coloured wallpaper and carpets, and the reproductions of engravings by Bohuslav Reynek, more or less everywhere, on the shelves, the doors – wonderful images from the *Snow* cycle, and from *Job*, *The Passion*, *Don Quixote*. Brum had always been a great admirer of Reynek, whose work as a translator he thought of as highly as his poetry and engravings. They were inspired pieces of work imbued with light, like a garden illuminated at twilight by a cherry tree in blossom; penetrated with silence, like a forest landscape lying under snow; and dazzled by a vision of intense gentleness, like one whose lips and eyelids are brushed, in sleep, by an angel. Above all, Brum had liked the man, the recluse of Petrkov in such profound harmony with the earth and the seasons, in such clear sympathy with man and beast; who listened to language with such sensitivity, and kept such long and attentive vigil on the brink of the invisible. And for the first time Ludvik realized how similarly in essence these two men had lived their lives.

In T, the snow still lay deep and hardened. And it was on this snow, within the walls of the cemetery, that the ashes of Joachym Brum were scattered. They cast only a delicate shadow, like that of the birds the little boy in the mountains fed with salt. But there was no child here to offer a gift of salt and express a welcome. There was Eva, dressed all in black, a few old folk, and Ludvik. All they threw was a handful of flowers, sorry-looking glasshouse flowers, pale and scentless, whose petals would be soon ruined by the frost. Ludvik remembered what the child had said about the salt: 'Well, I scatter it over everything I love as a gesture of welcome into my memory, of invitation into my heart.' Ludvik would so much have liked the little boy to be there, at that very moment, to give Brum a peaceful send-off, Brum who was no more than ashes now, ashes already dissolving in the snow crystals. Brum who was gone from the earth, carried away by the wind, the wind that took the place of singing, a psalm without words, a breath whistling across the face of the sky.

Having exchanged a few words and hugs with Eva, the mourners left, and Ludvik found himself alone beside her at the cemetery gate. She was more taciturn than ever. Ludvik dared not voice his desire to visit Linden Street, so he invited her to have lunch with him in a restaurant, if she felt like it. She hesitated for a moment, then said she was not really hungry, and certainly didn't want to be surrounded by people, but she invited him to come back to her place.

They walked down an avenue lined with ash trees,

then caught a trolley-bus that took them to the corner of Linden Street. When they reached the foot of the building, Ludvik looked up at the windows of Brum's living-room. They were gleaming as usual. Eva had not failed in her houseproud fastidiousness. Climbing the stairs behind her, he thought that in fact the whole of Eva's life could be summoned up in these terms: she was a silent and austere homemaker. Brum was the gentle genius of the place.

They took off their coats in the hall. Eva was dressed in a black jumper and straight skirt. Mourning accentuated her thinness and the severity of her features. Ludvik thought she looked like a charcoal-coloured crane, as he followed her down the corridor whose floor creaked. He also noticed the sounds had a peculiar sonority, the kind created by empty space. And when he crossed the threshold into the living-room he was dazzled by the light: the sun flooded through the curtainless windows, splashed the bare and yellowed walls, rippled over the pale waxed floorboards. There remained not a single piece of furniture, knick-knack, book, or carpet. The living-room was empty. Eva, noticing Ludvik's amazement, explained. She was moving. Under the terms of the restitution laws, the whole building had reverted to the ownership of someone who had decided to undertake major renovation works, as a result of which the rents were going to increase and she was unable to assume such expense. In any case this apartment was too big for her, now that she was left on her own, and the absence of her uncle, whom she always called by his first name, Joachym, was all too tangible. She had anticipated this day when she would have to leave, give up this place where she had lived for so long, and she had prepared her retreat. She was going back to where she had started out from, to her native village in Moravia. She stated the facts briefly, in a detached tone of voice, without adding the least commentary or revealing any distress or nostalgia.

'But do you still have family there?' asked Ludvik.

'Some distant cousins, with whom I haven't really kept in contact. I left such a long time ago. I was just fifteen when my parents died, killed in a car accident. It was then that my uncle Joachym took me in.'

Eva did not waive her obligations as mistress of the house, even though the place had been emptied of furniture. She managed to find an old stool and a folding chair, then went off to the kitchen to fill a kettle. The move had taken place the previous week, she had kept only a few things, just enough to camp with until her own departure, scheduled for the following day. She had only stayed on for the cremation. She improvised a picnic in the living-room, laid out on top of a suitcase some tomatoes cut into quarters, a piece of cheese, some bread and apples, all served on paper plates, then she brought out two mugs filled with Turkish coffee, apologizing for only being able to offer such meagre fare. They ate in silence. Outside a few birds uttered shrill cries, clustered notes. Eva sat against the light, very straight-backed, on the folding chair. Her features were almost indistinguishable, the blackness of her silhouette was all that made any impression. Brum's absence blended with the bright moted light gleaming on the floor, with the strident cries of the birds in the street. Brum's death was distilled in his niece's rigid black head and shoulders.

Eva, who was about to raise a piece of tomato to her lips, suspended her gesture and, turning her head slightly towards the windows, she said, 'Joachym often said that he would like to die one spring morning, in the brightness of day, to the chirping of returning birds. It happened otherwise. He died in the depths of winter, after nightfall.'

At these words Ludvik started and without any further hesitation he asked, 'By the way, Eva, what exactly did you mean by that date your uncle supposedly chose, decided on, as his dying day, even before he was dying. You alluded to it several times in the course of his illness . . .'

She slowly let her hand drop to the plate on her lap, but without moving her head, which remained in profile. 'I don't know any more about it than he did. Mere conjecture.'

'Not really,' Ludvik insisted, 'when you mentioned that date on the telephone you seemed rather sure . . .'

'Yes and no.'

'But that date turned out to be correct . . .' Ludvik hazarded.

'Yes, he died on the anticipated date,' she finally consented.

Then Ludvik immediately specified, 'The anniversary of an event dating back four hundred years to which no one, or virtually no one, attributes any importance now.'

Eva turned her face towards him and looked him straight in the eye, but without showing any surprise or asking any questions. As she continued to remain silent, Ludvik went on.

'Well, why was he so interested in that meeting between the Emperor Rudolph and the Maharal of Prague? It was an important event, of course, but all the same . . . So many other things have happened since that day, to the Hradsin of Prague, and everywhere else in the world, why that day more than any other?'

Eva tilted her head towards one shoulder and looked down at the piece of tomato she still held in her fingers. 'It seems absurd, I admit, and yet you worked out what the date was. You knew as well. So it must mean that in spite of everything there is some sense in it.'

Ludvik was about to cut in, to tell her that he had eventually worked it out, albeit in retrospect, solely because she had put him on the trail by means of her many hints, for all their vagueness, and because a tangle of coincidences, hunches, had gradually led him to this hypothesis, when she added, 'But it's no surprise that you should have found out the date, Joachym mentioned it in the notebook I gave you the last time you came. He'd long been interested in that event. In fact I expected you to raise the subject much earlier . . .'

Ludvik felt himself redden at the thought of the lost notebook, and catching his breath, he retorted, 'You do have a way of reversing the situation! You made such veiled, vague allusions to this date, during our brief telephone conversations, I thought it better not to insist . . .'

With a flick of her hand, Eva continued with what she was saying. 'What difference does it make? Anyway, neither you nor I can give a rational explanation for it. Besides, reason has very little place in all this. Reason! Our age has so much abased reason, it has done such injury to our consciences! Joachym could never espouse the cause of this century, reeking with the smell of charnel houses, choking him, catching in his throat like a sob. But he never laid down arms in his quest for some meaning, he never stopped groping, for as long as he could, wherever he could, through the fog tainted with blood, sweat and tears of blood, that has shrouded our times. In his wanderings he found this halo of brightness, the trace left by two men who met secretly, on the fringes of their own age's frenzy, and so in the very heart of the chaos of those days. At the approach of death, he made that little halo, as distant as it was legendary, his guiding light. After all, doesn't the light of the stars travel for thousands upon thousands of years before reaching our celestial space? The more you participate in your own age, and the more you inhabit the present, then the more you exist out of time, in manifold time.'

She paused, raised the tomato quarter, its pulp glistening, to the level of her face, then put it back on her plate again, and dusted off the few crumbs that had fallen onto her skirt. Ludvik had rarely heard her talk so much. It was as though Brum's words and expressions were restored to life through her. She soon resumed her dual-voiced monologue with unexpected expansiveness and ease.

'Yes, reason's not what we're dealing with here, it's passion rather. For it must surely have been a matter of passion. A long and austere passion of conscience, of heart and soul. An infinite compassion, which crystallized round an event of apparently minor significance, but sufficiently important to supplant in him his desire to die in the springtime. In fact I don't know whether it was his illness that brought on this crisis of anxiety within him, such that it eventually turned into an internal disaster, or whether it was this latent anxiety that was responsible for his illness. A confused vortex.

'As he gradually lost the thread of his memory and the use of words, I saw the resurgence within him of that terror for his century, the reopening of that wound inflicted on reason. The more that memories of his own existence frayed, the more penetrating became that disquieted mind. From the depths of his armchair, and then his bed, he began to dwell maniacally on these questions as old as humanity. Why are the just always thwarted? Why are hopes always disappointed? Why are so many innocents for ever being mistreated, put to death, amid general indifference and deceitfulness? Why should it always be the violent, the powerful, the arrogant, who triumph and prevail?

'One day, when he was sitting in his armchair by that window there, I saw him throw aside with rage the newspaper he was reading. It was a September afternoon, the weather was fine, the living-room was bathed with light. As he threw the paper on the floor, he said to himself, “Enough of this!” The tone of his voice surprised me; a tone so muffled, so choked with anger, distress . . . I asked him what was wrong. He didn’t answer. I went over to him, but he seemed neither to see nor hear me. Then he got up and retired to his room, telling me he felt tired and wanted to rest a little.

‘When I knocked on his door towards evening, to find out if he was feeling better and wanted any supper, there was no response. I was worried. I opened the door a fraction, without making any noise. He was lying on his bed, with his eyes wide open, staring into space. I entered the room, went over to his bed, and saw that his face was streaming with tears. But he seemed not to be aware that he was weeping. I sat at his bedside, and took his hands in mine. They were freezing cold and trembling. His lips too were trembling. I wiped his tear-stained face. Bending very close, I heard him murmuring, though with his jaws still clenched.

‘He said that he had lived through this century without any realization of the evil that reigned; he was ashamed to be so old when millions of children had been robbed of life. And he kept repeating that a fire had just blazed in his heart, the great fire relentlessly ignited by the horde of brutes who had swept across the world, and continued to rampage, that he could smell the burning of books, all the books he had ever read, reflected on, loved, throughout his life, the burning of words, poems, the burning of the words of others, the burning of laughter and songs, the burning of language. The horror of evil was intense within him, and nothing of all that he might have read, learned, loved, was enough to appease him. Language had fallen prey to the flames, in his flesh, in his heart . . .

'That night he had his first attack. When he came back from the hospital, he could only speak with great difficulty. He would remain in his armchair for hours, reduced to utter dejection. At first I read to him, books that he liked, or certain articles, but he very quickly let me know this wasn't what he wanted. He would flap his one good hand abruptly, as if to chase away some bothersome insect. Yet one day, with that hand, he pointed out to me a book on the shelf. I hurried to fetch it, and brought it to him. He leafed through it until he found the page he was looking for. Precisely the one referring to that meeting we spoke of, between Emperor Rudolph and Rabbi Loew. He placed a finger on that passage and uttered a few words in his broken, almost inaudible voice. "I shall find out, I shall find out what they said to each other that day. I shall be there on that day." Then he closed the book. And I realized then that he had just decided on the day he would die.'

'And what book was that?'

'I don't know. At the time I only paid attention to the few lines he had been reading, trying to understand what he was saying, his speech was slurred . . . Then I must have put the book back on the shelf. And as he had several on the subject of the Maharal of Prague, and the age of Rudolph II, and as he covered all his books in brown paper, I forgot which one it was. But that doesn't really matter. What I did remember was the date he mentioned, which he intended to be his last, for he'd just abruptly announced to me that the countdown to his death was now inexorably underway. And for the following five months, time was condensed into an hour-glass, and I knew with painful precision how many its grains of sand numbered. One hundred and fifty-nine days exactly. As for the book, I shall have unlimited time to find it when I'm settled in my new home, and I've unpacked the boxes. But that all seems of very minor importance to me right now.'

'Yet it's not ... didn't you just tell me how much he suffered, suddenly feeling all those books burning inside him? So this one book survived the great fire that broke out in his heart? This one only!'

'It wasn't so much the book as the event it described, which interested him ... in fact, I think that event, however fascinating in itself, only obsessed him to such an extreme because it fitted into a much broader context, like a brilliant comma in the chaotic and obscure account of history, like a point of suspension, a momentary pause in which to draw breath, a lull in which gleamed a promise of meaning, or a very fine question mark ... in short, an essential punctuation. Joachym was no more an historian, or religious specialist, than he was a philosopher. Just a man enamoured of meaning, of justice ... a man tragically tormented with hope, in the face of everything, until the very end.'

'And now that he's dead, does he finally know what he so yearned to find out?'

'Am I acquainted with the mysteries of the dead?' said Eva, looking at him directly. 'I was barely acquainted with that of Joachym while he was alive, and I lived with him all my adult life. I've come to doubt that anyone is acquainted with the mystery of their own self. The distress that so violently overwhelmed Joachym in the months preceding his death is also connected with this lack of knowledge. He suddenly found himself haunted by questions with which he had certainly never ceased to be preoccupied, but from a distance, approaching them obliquely, by ways whose beauty exalted everything. And suddenly those ways came to a dead end, they caught fire, they ended in total nothingness. He didn't know that he was so involved in the tragedies of his age, he didn't know how great the demands on him were, of this torment, this wounded love for men, mortified by its own powerlessness.'

'Was he a believer? He often spoke, in the past, of the divine, but in the same way as the poets that affected him most speak of it. He said nothing of God.'

'What could he have said? What can any of us say? A person needs to be truly inspired or else very daring to talk of God.'

'But the dialogue that took place four centuries before his death, and on which he concentrated his lasting remaining powers of attention, of thought, must have considered the mystery of creation, plumbed the resonance of that extremely problematic name, God. It was nevertheless that dialogue, and no other, that he wanted to hear. So?'

Ludvik was also seized with an urgent need to understand, and he now obstinately asked questions that he had always dismissed as irrelevant. But as over the course of recent months he gradually lost his few certainties and landmarks, and reality seemed to shift, like drift-ice breaking up, he found himself cast into a new and unfamiliar setting whose laws and logic, however absurd, he tried blunderingly to work out. And then he felt so disorientated in this empty living-room streaming with honeyed straw-coloured light, before a woman in black proving to be so different from his conception of her. He had to try to mark out this turbulent wilderness with beacons.

'So what?' said Eva in an almost harsh tone of voice. 'I told you, I'm not acquainted with the mysteries of the dead. Nor those of God. I don't like talking about things of which I am completely ignorant. Anyway, with Joachym, it was above all silence that we shared. A bent for silence, for listening to the silence.' She ceased talking, and so they remained for a long moment.

'Would you like more coffee?' she suddenly asked in a softened voice, as if waking from a light and furtive slumber.

'No, thank you. It's time I was leaving. I imagine you still have a lot to do,' said Ludvik, getting to his feet. 'But if I can be of any help . . .'

'Thank you, that's very kind of you, but there's no need. Everything's already prepared, and all in order.'

She too stood up, and added with a smile conveying a little sadness and bitterness, 'I've always been a woman of order. More now than ever before.'

'You say that in a tone of regret,' remarked Ludvik, who wished he could comfort her, and above all express the sympathy and respect she suddenly inspired in him, after so many years of indifference and even vague scorn. 'You are indeed a woman of order, but in the deepest, most inward sense of the term. Or the most elevated, it comes to the same thing. A sense in which I'm lacking.'

'Great disorder may in the end turn out to be equally productive, who knows?' she said, slightly shrugging her shoulders.

They stood facing each other. Ludvik could not distinguish Eva's features very well against the light, he could only see the gleam of her eyes. A contained, powerful gleam.

'By the way,' she exclaimed suddenly, 'I was about to forget . . .' And she walked across the room, went into the hall from where she returned with her handbag. A big black canvas bag with a strap trimmed with tobacco-coloured leather. 'I'd put aside a book for you, which Joachym was very fond of, one of his bedside books. It isn't in very good condition any more, he so often leafed through it! He knew its contents by heart. I put it in my bag because I didn't know whether you'd leave straight after the ceremony or whether you'd stay a while . . .'

As she rummaged in her bag, Ludvik felt himself redden again, and he felt giddy for a moment. He was rehearsing a scene that had already been played out, almost identically, a few months earlier, at the time of his last visit. He was expecting Eva to hand him a brown paper envelope, to give him back the lost notebook – and to send him away with harsh words.

Had time gone into reverse, had these last months been only a temporal illusion, was Brum still alive, was it all nothing but a dream? A dream, but then who was dreaming about whom?

'Ah, here it is!' said Eva, producing a thin, rather large-sized package, wrapped in a sheet of newspaper.

Ludvik remained motionless, his arms hanging loosely at his side, his heart thumping. He dared not reach out for this new package, as if it would disintegrate at his touch. He dared not break the uneasy spell of that moment in which time was suspended.

'Well, take it!' Eva insisted. 'After nearly thirty years in the hands of its recipient, the book's returning to its sender.'

Ludvik stared at her, widening his eyes, comprehending nothing of what she said.

'This book', she added, 'is one that you gave to Joachym, towards the end of your student days. You bought it from a dealer in the Old Town.'

'Really? I don't remember . . .'

'It was such a long time ago now, you must have forgotten. Joachym was very fond of this book, he said it was a link between him and you. I'm returning it to you, so that it remains a link, in reverse. The sender has become the recipient.'

Ludvik stammered out his thanks, turning the package over in his hands. Eventually, he stuffed it into the pocket of his overcoat, cast a final glance over the empty living-room from which the light was beginning to fade.

Eva accompanied him to the front door. On the threshold, he offered her his hand, which she took. Then they both started, indiscernibly, and gazed at each other in astonishment. It had been so many years since they last shook hands. Eva was always in the habit of greeting him from a distance, with her arms crossed, close to her chest, and with a slight inclination of her head. As it was, she immediately shrank back, almost imperceptibly, and withdrew her hand, then gave a wan smile. Ludvik smiled in return, even more faintly. He wished there was something he could say, but he was unable to think of anything. He stood wavering, in the doorway, lowered his eyes, then walked away. Without a sound, she closed the door behind him.

VOLTE-FACE

He had more than three hours to wait until his train left. So he sauntered through the streets of T, then went into a café. He took the parcel from his pocket, laid it on the table and unwrapped the newspaper around it. Stuck on the cover was a reproduction of Paul Klee's 'Ad Marginem', in the centre of which floats a purple sun, with a strange little bird stuck above it, upside down, with its feet in the air. He turned the book over. On the back was another Klee reproduction, 'Le Fou de l'abîme', whose red face against a night background, gives a faint humorous smile, while at the same time shedding a big red tear. Eventually he opened the book. Written on the half-title was a dedication in faded ink: 'For Joachym Brum, whose nomadic mind scatters the words of poets like so many glittering salt-crystals, sunrays, and moonbeams. With respect and gratitude, Yours Ludvik.' He turned the page and came to the title page. It was an anthology of French poetry of the first half of the twentieth century.

Brum certainly did not need to wait for one of his young students to offer him this work in order to discover Paul Fort, Francis Jammes, Blaise Cendrars, Guillaume Apollinaire, Jules Supervielle, and the surrealists, he must have read their works even long before. So why had he attached so much importance to this work, and granted it a privileged place, at least according to what Eva had said? Could it be that he felt such great affection for his fervent pupil of the past? But Ludvik had soon lost that fervour, and Brum must have been offended, or disappointed, if not hurt. No, in Ludvik's view, he was really not worthy of the fact that a little book he had once given as a present should be faithfully preserved like a relic by the recipient of the modest gift. He leafed through the anthology and came across a collage made on a piece of cardboard the size of postcard, serving as a page-marker. Yet another montage created by Ludvik, who recalled that he sometimes used to amuse himself with this kind of thing in his student days – cutting up images and texts, turning them upside down, like the little bird in Paul Klee's painting, setting them at variance, in motion, in rotation.

This collage featured a vast sky, cut out of the clouds of El Greco's 'View of Toledo', a landscape consisting of rocky outcrops with steep slopes taken from a Giotto fresco, and walking through this desert of rock and rolling sky, three very tall thin figures, with enormous feet, the heel of one striking the sky and the sole of the other bearing down on the ground. Meticulously cut-out silhouettes of Giacometti's statues. Ludvik turned the card over. It was more recent than the book in which it served as a page-marker, it dated from the time when he decided to emigrate. He read the few lines he had written to Brum at the time by way of farewell.

'They, the living ones, have been on the move for such a long time, and we, so stationary. I've waited only too long, I'm afraid of losing sight of them.

Isn't all wandering a chance we must know how to take, just as you taught me? It's high time I left. Hoping that we'll be given the opportunity to meet again one day, I bid you farewell, with affection, Ludvik.'

He laid the card on the open page. Shame overwhelmed him, acute and chilling, because he was confronted with himself. The last time he visited Brum, he had judged him on his decrepit physical appearance – a senile old man, who had lost his memory and power of speech. A wreck that life had thrown aside. Yet that old man had kept his memory intact, and his mind vigilant, whereas Ludvik had forgotten everything: the book he had given as a present when he was young, the dedication, the Paul Klee images stuck on the cover, and the card he had sent as a final message before leaving the country.

He had forgotten everything, been remiss in everything, got everything wrong. And now suddenly Joachym Brum, the man who had become a handful of ashes that had melted into the snow, was restoring his past, his memory, lifting his heart, his spirit, raising them like a standard in the wind. Joachym Brum, the man already gone from this earth, with no tomb other than that of his niece's love, was urging him to set out again, to rediscover a taste for life, however bitter or sour that taste might be. Bitter, and yet intense, persistent. Joachym Brum, approaching eternity by going backwards in time, on his quest to find meaning in the invisible, continuing to open tombs for himself in the hearts and minds of the living, vast empty tombs, glittering with another light. Joachym Brum, the infinitely generous recipient who returned the least gift, the least word, multiplying it, magnifying it.

Ludvik put the card back at the page where he had found it, among the verses of the poem 'Cortège' by Guillaume Apollinaire, which he glanced over, and closed the book. He searched his memory, but succeeded in excavating only a very poor recollection: he saw himself rummaging through boxes full of old books that gave off a stale smell of dust and yellowed paper at a bookseller's on Mala Strana, where he often went browsing in his youth. A shop that had long since disappeared, replaced first of all by a fruit and vegetable shop, and, recently, by a gift shop selling tee shirts printed with idiotic phrases and grotesque caricatures of Kafka, Mozart, the Golem, or even lewd piglets, skulls, or portraits of stars and idols. From books to comic-strip clothing, via leeks, cabbages and potatoes. But after all, was not the collage assembly of El Greco's sky, Giotto's rocks, and Giacometti's walking figures, in its own way, a comic strip, briefly recounting an endless story? The story of each and every one of us, for ever starting anew: of walking, day after day, here on earth, defying weight and immobility, following the paths of time, dream and reality, searching the night and the light, listening to the voice of the wind, the words of others, the secret song of the earth, the cries of history, the indistinct sound of our own blood fraught with so many mysteries, echoes and questions. A story of which Ludvik had some intimation, but which he had blocked out, while Brum had read, interpreted, translated it, in his flesh, and lived it from beginning to end.

He looked at his watch. There was still a good hour before he had to be at the station. He felt a desire to go back and see Eva, he had so many questions to ask her, about this book, and the lost notebook, and the card Brum had written at Christmas, when he was already bedridden. She must have read that card, no one but she could have posted it, she surely knew things that she was keeping to herself, or at least understood better than he did the underlying pattern woven into their lives, beneath the appearance of accident and absurdity glittering on the surface.

He thought back to the legend of the angel of acquaintance Katia had told him about. At the time, he had only been able to relate that story to his broken liaison with Esther – a great love affair that ended badly and a totally routed angel. But that angel, no matter how far it had fallen, no matter what injury it had suffered, must still exist somewhere in the insubstantial realms of time, for whatever has occurred cannot be obliterated, nothing that one day existed can be denied, disguised as nothing. Every instant of the past remains part of the substance of the present, a rich and humble sediment, a tiny nugget of light, endlessly resmelted and gleaming in secret in the depths of oblivion. Ludvik sensed his past stirring and rising within him, an assembly of more or less luminous or shadowy transparencies: the angels born of all the acquaintances he had made throughout his life. And among them, very frail and remarkable, the angel of his relationship with Brum.

Ludvik walked at a rapid pace to Linden Street, but as soon as he got there, he lost his nerve. He started to slow down even from the corner of the street, suddenly overcome with qualms and irresolution, and he stood there, on the pavement, in front of the building, looking up at the windows of Brum's living-room.

Brum, the departed, in his absence so present, whispering so much in his silence, now rose before Ludvik, confronted him, in an incongruous, disconcerting manner, in the albeit very banal façade of the house where he had lived. As if this façade were a funereal stele erected in honour of Brum, a tombstone standing vertically against the sky. And Ludvik could not cross the thoroughfare, enter the tomb, for all of a sudden he sensed how pointless it was to come back and haunt this place. Brum was so much elsewhere, and Eva was leaving. And besides, had not everything already been said? What more could he expect?

He remained on the street, feeling drained, lost in contemplation of the façade.

Daylight was fading, the sun was no longer reflected by the windows and there was no light on inside. The tall windows looked like unsilvered mirrors, slightly blue-tinged in the semi-darkness of twilight. Pages of glass on which only the evening wind traced invisible signs. And Ludvik's thoughts drifted, to the rhythm of the blue-tinged wind. Write, then erase, read, forget, speak, and then fall silent, love, and consent not to be loved any more, seize, then let go – love, and remain true, know, and not comprehend anything. And in the end, wait. Wait empty-handed, with a heart laid bare and an open mind, without even being able to name what it is you wait for, with infinite patience, extreme endurance. Like Joachym Brum, who fell on a field of honour, of tragic intimacy, immense humanity.

Some of the words uttered by the hospital cleaner returned to him in a subdued echo: 'What do we know of the hidden tears of others? . . . All these tears form stalactites that break on the day we die . . . all these tears exuded by the salt of oblation . . . '

The windows grew darker and darker, acquiring an obsidian blackness. And suddenly they were splashed with light, returned to their former transparency. A slender shadow moved across them: Eva was walking through the living-room. She was carrying something in her hands at chest level. Ludvik could not make out what that object was – a receptacle of some kind, a serving dish, or a bowl, perhaps. The image that had for some time been appearing to him in visions, at once sudden, slow and haunting, the image of the three Magi walking in slow motion through an ashen desert, then resurfaced in his mind. Eva had the same bearing, a gaunt queen, robed in darkness from head to foot, reigning over a desert of resounding silence. What was she carrying, cupped in her hands – the radiance of that silence, her uncle's tears, the fire and salt of those tears? Or her own solitude burnished by patience? Or else, Ludvik wondered, in a crazy leap of imagination, or else, what if it were his heart that Eva was carrying in her thin hands, up there in the deserted living-room? His heart, or at least a tiny fragment of his heart that he had lost without being aware of it, during their conversation that afternoon?

He stood there, on the pavement, his face still upturned towards the lighted windows. Eva's silhouette glided from one to the other, a shadow queen in exile, a shadow Magus against a golden background. And his mind went into a state of weightlessness, started to drift. He was floating in an inner no-man's-land, as if washed out, inwardly depleted, by the woman with the broom. He felt dispossessed of himself, infiltrated by presences other than his own, and other absences too.

Suddenly the light went out, darkness returned, engulfing Eva, the living-room, the pale fire of Brum's tears, and a part of himself. He shivered, overtaken by the cold and by nightfall, and he stuffed his hands into his pockets, but remained at his lookout post, though all he could see was a façade in total shadow, barely distinguishable from the violet-brown sky.

Standing behind the window in the gloom of the living-room, Eva observed Ludvik blindly keeping watch down below on the pavement. She had noticed him as she walked across the room, carrying a ceiling lamp-globe she had just taken down in order to wash the grimy dust off it. Surprised at first by Ludvik's presence in the street so long after he had left the apartment, then disturbed by the persistence of this presence that was as discreet as it was unusual, she paced the living-room several times, still holding the lampshade in her hands, and finally went and switched off the light, so that she could come and gaze in the dark on this peculiar sentry. What did he want? What was he waiting for? Nothing, maybe.

'No,' she said to herself, 'it can't be me that he's watching out for, like that. He doesn't care about me. He's dreaming, asleep on his feet. A somewhat tired old horse feeling a momentary touch of nostalgia. Joachym's death may grieve him a little after all. Or else he may just want to take one last look at a place he'll have no reason to return to any more. He doesn't realize he's staring at me, without seeing me . . . but he's never really seen me . . . and he's unequally unaware that I'm looking at him. It's all of so little importance now. Even so, this is a strange farewell . . . '

The street lamps came on, casting a dull yellow brightness. Ludwik was standing between two lamp posts, suffused with a faint halo of straw-coloured light. From up above, behind the dark windows, it was difficult to distinguish his features. Eva guessed at rather than saw them, reconstructing his face on the basis of her familiarity with it, a little imagination distorting this reconstruction. Ludvik removed his hands from his pockets and raised them to his collar, which he buttoned and turned up.

Then her recollection of a scene, suppressed for nearly thirty years, suddenly broke loose from the limbo of oblivion, of denial, rising from her memory in all its rawness, and imposing itself on her consciousness.

Her recollection of an evening when her love was brought crashing down, when her youth keeled over into cold indifference to her age, to the impulses of desire. At that time Eva was not yet living in T. She and Joachym were still based in the capital. It was not until a few years later that Brum withdrew to the provinces, after he had been forced out of the university and into retirement. Eva, a young woman beyond the reach of time or desire, had followed her already aged uncle.

The scene that now replayed in her memory had taken place in a corridor, behind a door. The corridor was in darkness, and the door was glazed, lit from within. The glazing consisted of thick panels of orange-yellow tinted glass. Eva used to tell her boyfriend that his lodgings made her think of a solar aquarium. But that evening the partition was more like a kaleidoscope of sickening outrageous beauty, a beauty as brutal as a slap across the face.

At the door, with one hand already touching the door knob, and the other about to knock at the glass panes, Eva suspended her actions at the very last moment. Through the wall of the aquarium she had just glimpsed an unfamiliar figure moving with languour. Everything inside her was arrested, her thoughts, her breathing, her senses, everything except her eyes. Her eyesight actually sharpened suddenly, as if concentrating all her energy, all her powers of attention.

In the orange glow of the bedroom was a dark-haired girl sitting cross-legged on the bed, a few paces behind the glass. And the girl was naked, screamingly beautiful, heartbreakingly shameless. Eva should have left immediately, run away from that obscene window, or she could have broken open the door, banged on the glass, but it was too late, right from the start. Amazement had turned her to stone. What she saw was too powerful, it compelled Eva's gaze. The girl sat in majesty like some carnal idol, slick with light.

The idol was lasciviously swaying her head, her shoulders, arching, thrusting forward her belly, her heavy breasts, then hunching her back in a slow rhythm. Now and then, raising her hands, she lifted her hair to the nape of her neck, then opened her arms again and slid them down the small of her back. Two more arms occasionally extended from behind her shoulders. Eva watched all these arms waving like an octopus's tentacles. A huge honey-coloured octopus.

A two-headed octopus. A tousled fairer head slowly rolled from one of the girl's shoulders across to the other, then dipped behind her back, soon to reappear amid the mass of tawny curls. The blonde head nestled against the idol's neck, nuzzled her ears, the nape of her neck. And the girl gave a little burst of joyful laughter, which then died out in a languishing sigh.

An eight-limbed creature. Two more legs had emerged from the girl's hips, slipped beneath her thighs, locked round her ankles. She arched, threw back her head and drew up her quadruple knees that gleamed like pebbles. The entwined legs parted, slowly, as wide as possible. Then two hands appeared from the girl's armpits, then climbed to her breasts, lingered there, caressing them, and then those hands slowly crept down to her belly, her groin, and there the fingers grew frenzied, playing in the dark bush before venturing into the heart of this jet triangle cleft with a crimson oval, and parting the edges of it.

Eva had no knowledge of the secrets of her own body, and here they were revealed to her, crudely, almost cheerfully, through the semi-transparent wall of a solar aquarium, in the body of a much more attractive and more sensual girl than she was. An octopus girl who opened her thighs and offered up her genitalia in all nonchalance and joyful shamelessness. When she herself had opened and offered up nothing but her heart, in all trustfulness and fervent simplicity.

Frozen behind the glass panel, she watched those hands, the hands of that other person pressed against the octopus girl's back, hands that explored the moist flesh of that oval, in folds of flushed and swollen rosiness, like some marine flower opening the fleshy petals round its heart, a little sunken heart fringed with darkness. The hands buried their fingers in that groove. The girl lifted herself up a little and a very hardened penis stood erect beneath her, then plunged deep into that heart, a rose in full bloom. Then the hands clung to the girl's hips, breasts, arms, hair, hips again, belly, sides, and she was not laughing or sighing any more, but moaning, sometimes crying out, while dancing on the spot, half squatting, shaking her head in sudden fits and starts. She was performing a bizarre dance, at once beautiful and ugly, Eva could not have said which; a violent dance, reduced to jerks of her entire body, still under assault from those hands that seemed to multiply and increase their frenzy, their speed, and which grabbed hold of it in the most carnal way to accelerate the tempo of its judderings. A savage idol, maddened with nakedness, rhythm and panting. And suddenly the octopus idol arched violently, uttered a twofold cry – one rising shrilly, the other a raucous expulsion, and the colours of the scene blended with these sounds in Eva's crazed eyes. Resonant, hallucinated eyes. The shrill cry glittered bright yellow, the raucous cry was steeped in purple, dark brown and violet. The girl exulted in the orange light, in the pearly glow of her inhabited flesh, the other was engulfed in the ardent obscurity within that flesh. Then the twofold cry died away and the idol's body slowly fell on to its side – a dual side, panting like that of a wounded beast. And yet again Eva's eyes were blinded by the sight of those dorsal hands, one resting in that dark hair, the other dangling from the shoulder of the girl, who had folded her arms over her breast and lay curled up in sensual satisfaction.

Eva stared at those hands left lying on the idol's body – the hands of the man she loved, and which she had only ever dared to squeeze tightly and occasionally brush with chaste kisses. The sacred hands of the man she loved and in which she had placed her dreamy innocent's heart. Treacherous, desecrated hands.

Eva finally regained control of herself, turned on her heels and left, without a sound and without looking back. It was a November evening, the wind was chasing rust-coloured leaves along the pavements. The colour of rust, mud, perfidy, like those unfaithful hands. The leaves raced along, crept over the asphalt, sometimes went into a brief whirl, then dropped down again, scattered. Eva stamped on these dead leaves, those limp hands. Those hands that had just prostituted their caresses before her eyes. In fact, what had she seen other than those hands? Not once had she seen the man's face, always hidden behind the girl's flesh-in-excessiveness, or in her hair. Neither had she noticed the girl's face. Only the gleam of her eyes, her teeth, her pudenda, in brief flashes. An idol has no face, it is a superabundance of flesh, limbs, genital organs, it blazes with shamelessness, with falsehood, but it is without a face. And by having identified himself with that idol, and become one with it, Ludvik had defiled himself in the intransigent eyes of Eva, whose love life had ended then, before even having really begun.

And Ludvik stood there, down below on the pavement, between two pools of pale light, with his bare hands crossed in front of his neck. Eva had seen him again over the course of the last thirty years, but always from a far remove, from the coldness of that distance she had established and whose magnitude she had never moderated or reduced, not even when the transgression was annulled by the lapse of time, and the scene was buried in oblivion – the scene that had just sprung to light again, resurfaced in her memory, and astounded her for the second time, but without upsetting her now. The days of young love, frenzies of virtue, passion and jealousy combined, were over. Life had gone on, following other paths, discovering other spaces on the heart's, mind's, soul's horizon. Life had gone on, slowly and solemnly, in silence and tranquillity. And this was just as well.

Eva watched Ludvik from the seclusion of the darkened window. Once again, this was a gaze from only one direction, a solitary vision. But a vision without violence, involving no rift or disgust. And no regret either. A reconciled vision. Like the one she had of Joachym dead.

A feeling of emptiness so amply suffused her body and mind that Eva relaxed her hands, still holding the lamp-globe. It fell at her feet, smashing on the floor. Was it the sound of breaking glass, shattering into fragments, or the flood of emptiness within her that made her shiver? She then had a very long-delayed reaction. She undressed slowly, deliberately, throwing her clothes on the ground among the broken glass.

And Eva stood naked, with her shoulders very straight, behind the darkened windowpanes. At that moment Ludvik began to walk away, it was time for him to get back to the station. He caught the merest glimpse of a pale shape up above – the reflection of a cloud, or of the moon. After one last glance, he then set off.

Eva remained for a long time like that, standing nude in the cold of the living-room, motionless in the dark. It was not the nudity of a body in celebration, of exultant flesh, that she exposed, but that of a skin polished by silence, patience, and dreams. The soft white surface of her heart, quietened beyond anguish, regret, bitterness, grief. A nudity like that of her uncle Joachym whom she had laid out when he entered upon the mystery of transition towards the invisible, to appear as summonsed. A like divestment, a like renouncement of the self, of all possessions; and a very, very deep humility and chastity. A nudity of prayer, of whiteness and silence, a nudity of forgiveness and love of pure compassion. And it was to the darkness, descending on the roofs of the small town of T that she was soon to leave, descending on the roofs of all towns, that Eva offered up her nudity, like a small gift, the colour of the moon, to the solitude of every single human being.

And Ludvik hurried towards the station, through the streets and lanes of the snow-covered, already sleeping town, bathed in moonlight, with the whiteness of a woman's body, casting far and wide in a motionless gesture her extremely pure and disturbing nudity, falling lightly upon it. The whiteness of a woman's heart all silvered with ashes and contemplation; strewn with dead leaves grown translucid; blinded with amazment and grief.

Loudspeakers announced the arrival of the train at the station. But in which language did these loudspeakers express themselves? Although he understood the succinct message they delivered,

Ludvik listened with surprise to the crackling voice, as if it rose from the ends of the earth and the confines of time, or else resonated in a dream he was having while fully awake and conscious.

The train travelled through the mauve darkness. It rocked gently through an increasingly featureless landscape: storage depots, a few houses, garden patches covered in snow, dark orchards, and then fields, meadows pitted with pools of water, clumps of trees that had shed their leaves, and so much sky, so much moonlit cloud above so much land blue with snow.

The train travelled on, quietly murmuring, murmuring. It was the whispering of life, humming its very slow, very urgent, tune. Ludvik felt a peacefulness such as he had never known before, so peculiar, even paradoxical, was it. This profound sense of peace that he experienced gradually diffused in him an equal sense of alarm; he felt as though threatened with wonder, dazzled with apprehension, in a state of complete and incredible alertness.

Ludvik did not fall asleep, despite his tiredness, the emotions of the day, the monotonous rocking of the train. He was too much on tenterhooks to be able to doze off, possessed by an indefinable expectation. Yet there was nothing happening, but in this very nothing, in the ordinariness of the time and place, he sensed something extraordinary. And everything seemed wonderful, even the electric light in the ceiling, the dirty windows, the passing scraggy bushes along the embankment.

The train murmured its undertone, paid out its long cable of sound: a rope of sound entwined with the echo of distant voices, muted with darkness, ashen with snow, milky with tears and moonlight. And Brum's voice, more than any other, ran through in a basso continuo.

Brum's voice reciting a poem:

'Tranquil bird in reverse flight bird
That nests in the air
At the limit of where our sun already shines
Lower your second eyelid the earth dazzles you
When you raise your head . . .'

Ludvik increasingly confused the rattling of the train with Brum's whispering voice, and he felt forgetfulness quiver inside him, like ice melting. The murmured words came from a very long way back, in snatches.

'Tranquil bird in reverse flight bird
That nests in the air
At the limit of where already my memory
shines
Lower your second eyelid
Neither because of the sun nor because of the
earth
But for this oblong fire whose intensity will only
increase
Until one day it becomes the only light.'

Brum's voice drizzled in the night, against the window, his breathing became palpable, grained like skin. Ludvik listened. He listened in total self-forgetfulness, in extreme concentration, to that voice at once so distant and so intimate that penetrated the darkness, that breathed within him.

'One day
One day I was waiting for myself
I said to myself Guillaume it's time you came
So that I might at last know the person that I am
I who know others
I know them through the five senses and a few
more . . . '

Brum's voice softly delivered Apollinaire's lines, in his flesh, his blood, his conscience at its most alert and attentive. Ludvik was both guest and host of the poem's beauty, at once receiving and according hospitality. A visitor to the very beauty visiting him. The guest-host of a dream finding expression in the midst of reality.

'O people that I know
I just need to hear the sound of their footsteps
To be able to tell ever afterwards which way
they went
I just need all of those to consider myself
entitled
To bring back to life the others
One day I was waiting for myself
I said to myself Guillaume it's time you came
And at a lyric pace advanced those I love
And I was not among them.'

It rose from the depths, flooded in from the horizon, welled up from the darkness, emanated from the snow, from nowhere, everywhere, and reached into him, into his flesh and blood.

> 'Then there came on the earth a thousand white
>   tribes
> Every man of which carried a rose in his hand
> And the language they invented on the way
> I learned from their own lips and I speak
>   it still
> The cortège passed and I looked for my body
>   there
> All those that turned up and were not myself
> One by one brought the pieces of myself
> I was constructed little by little as a tower is
>   raised
> The people crowded round and I appeared
>   myself
> Formed of all the bodies and all things
>   human . . .'

Then, with the strength of so much beauty, steeped to the utmost in dream and reality combined, these words broke through the visible world. From the crowd of those passing white tribes in Apollinaire's 'Cortège', a giant stood out, filling the void, filling him with wonder.

A tall body of wood sudden loomed up in the middle of a flat landscape, dominated by a moving sky, through which the moon diffused its pale rippling light. Dressed in its winter rags, shiny with darkness, it stood very upright at the edge of the sky and the earth, at the border between darkness and light, and it bore its naked, rounded boughs very high in the cold silence. A dormant beech tree, that stood dreaming, with panache, of the long history of the wind, the song of the emptiness, the creaking of its wood, and the quiverings of its shadow lying on the snow, in the brightness of the night. A somnambulant beech tree.

With its denuded limbs, bristling with branches, with slender twigs glistening with frost, the tree seemed to be standing upside down, to have buried its crest in the earth and extended its roots up into the sky. A tree planted topsy-turvy, rooted in the immensity of the fluid, insubstantial sky, in which shadows and light constantly ebbed and flowed. A funambulist beech gliding along the tightrope of the clouds, drawing from the wind, from empty space, its sap and its beauty, its reason for being and its strength to grow.

But it was just a lightning vision. An acrobat beech tree. No sooner had it appeared, with its aerial roots gleaming in the moonshine, than it was gone. It looked as if it was running, over there, driven by a violent momentum, chased like a cloud, drawn by a distant summons. It raced away, it raced away, with its secret momentarily exposed.

This fleeting vision sufficed to topple Ludvik, in turn, who felt himself plummeting into the gaping void within him. And he was like that tree stripped of its leaves by winter, divested of his gloom-filled doubts, the mawkishness of his melancholy, his disgust with the world and himself. He was like the tree, chilled through with frost, with space and moonlight, completely dazzled with darkness, and running, running away, ahead of himself, far, far away from himself, to meet himself. A fugitive radiance skimming the sky, close to the earth's surface, amid the billowing clouds and swirling scrub.

The train kept up its murmur – the words of Apollinaire, the voice of Brum, the thumping of Ludvik's heart. A great wave of emotion swept through him, his heart went into dehiscence, like those dwarf pines on the tundra that before any other plant, any other living thing, even when snow and ice still obdurately cover the earth, sense the imminent approach of spring, and stand there, strange and solitary, and shake themselves in the colourless steppe, bearers of a promise frozen so long that no one believed in it any more.

The train slowed and after a few jolts halted in a small station. Ludvik noticed a man standing on the platform, level with his compartment, but some way back. He was bareheaded, carried no luggage, and stood very straight, not moving, with his arms dangling at his sides. He wore a gabardine raincoat that attracted Ludvik's curiosity: it looked exactly like the one stolen from him a few months' before on this very train. Ludvik studied the individual more closely. Then he was struck by another, much more disturbing resemblance. This man was his double, gazing at him with a grave, almost sorrowful expression.

They stared at each other in silence, similarly motionless, the whole time the train was stopped. A minute or two, a flash of eternity. Then the carriage jerked and began to move off. Ludvik also gave a start, and flattened his hands, his forehead against the glass, his gaze riveted to the man's face. The man did not stir, he merely turned his head towards Ludvik. Ludvik thought he glimpsed a faint smile. A smile in which detachment and compassion were combined.

The train had picked up its rhythm again and was speeding along the rails. Ludvik settled himself against the back of his seat, his face still turned towards the window. He met the gaze of his own reflection in the glass. And this gaze was at once his own and that of the man glimpsed the moment before on the platform. The same slightly sorrowful gravity, a similar expression of expectation, of patience. Ludvik no longer knew whether what he was looking at was really himself, or the other man, he did not recognize himself in the flagrancy of his own image. He reached his hand towards the glass and brushed with his fingertips the closed lips of his reflection. Then the lips parted and the mouth began to speak in a faint tenuous voice: 'Ludvik, Ludvik . . .'

The voice seemed not so much to be calling him, or naming itself, as imploring something. But Ludvik did not know what it was this voice entreated, he only sensed the infinite imploration it contained, and the quiet depths of its desperation. 'Look at me . . . ' whispered the reflection whose lips moved beneath Ludvik's fingers. This face reflected in the glass was suggestive of the very disturbing mystery of a shroud with an impression of the dead person's face imprinted on it that comes to life. Ludvik had strayed so far into the desert of amazement that no question was able to formulate itself in his mind; it was his own being that found itself thoroughly called into question, transformed into sheer inapparence, insane absence. He could no longer tell to whom this mirrored face belonged, a face that resembled him in every feature, but seemed to live by virtue of some other life, to derive from some other source than his own person.

The voice continued, speaking still in quiet anguish: 'Since the moment of your birth, I've appended myself to your breathing, your heart. I am the cry of your birth, of your memory before that cry. I've shared your every day, I've followed you step by step, in every move, and I've lain in every one of your nights. Often I have laid my hand on your shoulder, but you knew no better at the time than to shrug carelessly and brush away my hand, as one might brush away unsightly specks of dust. I've borne the burden of your pains and sorrows, and the ever heavier burden of your doubts. But the most overwhelming was that of your indifference, your disillusionment. I held, for you, in my palm a tiny shard of light, a splinter of silence, but you were always prey to so many false movements of the heart and mind, I never succeeded in planting this grain inside you . . . Ludvik, through being absent from yourself and sickened by everything, you lost sight of yourself, you lost heart, and you so misunderstood me, you so deprived yourself of love, you ended up casting me adrift, losing touch with yourself, turning away from others . . . Ludvik, I've been looking for you for so long and pining for you like a dog spurned by its master, I've been looking for you and blaming myself like a master who has lost his dog, I've been looking for you and calling you like a brother in search of his prodigal and neglectful sibling . . . Ludvik, it's so cold in your neglectfulness, so dark in your disenchantment, there's such hunger and thirst in your disregard for the mystery of this world . . . '

With his forehead pressed against the glass, resting on the forehead of his own reflection, which stared him straight in the eye, Ludvik listened with his fingertips to this quivering murmur. All his defences collapsed. He surrendered, at the end of a battle fought internally, without his knowledge, if not against his will. He surrendered to himself, the inapparence of the world, the miracle of reality, the fundamental reality of the dream.

All these whispered words that he perceived with his fingertips were not reproaches, they were confessions. He was confessing to himself. He recognized himself as singular and plural; a moving zone inhabited at once by emptiness and a multitude of voices, faces, gestures and footsteps; a body in perpetual confluence; flesh in reprieve, instilled with echoes, with telltale traces and gazes; an incomplete heart whose every heartbeat disseminated in the world's clamour a new point of suspension, an ephemeral point of contact between self and others, the living and the dead. None of this formulated itself in his mind, it was a gentle rush of consciousness that spread in chiaroscuro from his fingers into every recess of his body.

The train entered the station, the journey was over. But, no, it was not over, it was beginning, elsewhere and otherwise. Ludvik pulled away from the window, from which his reflection faded. A few drops of water beaded on the glass, a fine slow-moving trickle. Ludvik wiped his hand over the windowpane, the drops of water wet his fingers. He raised his hand to his lips, a slight taste of salt fizzed in his mouth.

He got off the train.

Ludvik: was that his name? Having been called that by the ghostly face whose forehead had pressed against his own, he did not know what his name was any more. Like those poems or paintings that appear under the indeterminate term 'Untitled', not because their author lacked imagination, but on the contrary, because he had transcended its bounds, and left the work free to expand in all directions, to extend beyond itself, Ludvik had the sense of floating in the unnamed, the unknown. And he felt a new childish happiness, for this floating was no longer aimless wandering but escape well away from his own being.

Without any title, without a name, relieved of his former melancholy and nostalgia, unburdened of all bitterness and finally unshackled of his indifference, he came at the deep of night into the morning light of the world. It did not much matter now where he was or which town he lived in. He had just entered another, boundless, space that extended further than the eye could see, beyond the limits of vision, to the outermost reaches of the spirit. A place where everything untangles and fans out, where questions are liberated of the need for answers, only to increase in their force of amazement; a place where thoughts break loose and run free, and the heart bares itself.

He crossed the concourse where travellers wandered about in the acid neon light, their eyes misted with cold and sleepiness: some bedded down for the night, with no luggage and no destination, their eyes burning with another kind of fever.

He emerged from the station. Outside an icy wind was blowing. Fine flurries of snow whirled in the amber-yellow halos of the street lamps. Despite the cold and the wind, he felt like walking. Cars glided slowly along the roadway, with a muffled sound. He walked down one avenue, then another, zigzagged across streets. He walked aimlessly, inhaling the smell of the stones, of the snow-covered asphalt. A tram came by. He hesitated and eventually got on it. For a while he sat back, watching the snow that kept falling, a thick scattering of silence over the torpid town. The tram branched off towards the river and ran along the embankment. A couple crossed the bridge, sheltering under a black umbrella. For a moment the pair executed a funny little dance step, then regained their balance. A pale crescent moon trembled in a breach in the sky, high above the rooftops, a translucid comma punctuating a purplish vortex with a brief pause; an indecisive pause reflected in the river above the bridge, where the umbrella wavered, like a big black bird hesitating to take flight.

He got off at the next stop. He cut across towards some narrow lanes where the snow and darkness condensed into crystals of dream and drifts of shadow. He zigzagged his way between brown façades on which atlantes kept vigil. Somewhere a dog barked; its barking was joyful, ringing out clear and light. Ludvik thought of a passage from 'The Fifth Well' in Rabbi Loew's *Well of Exile*, in which it is written that 'if the dogs howl, it is because the Angel of Death has entered town. If they laugh, it is because the Prophet Elijah has entered town.' Because, by the very fact that these animals number among the humblest and least of creatures, it is given to them to detect supernatural signs and spiritual presences that humans, imbued with a sense of their own superiority, rarely perceive.

'For the Prophet Elijah is the antithesis of the Angel of Death. From the latter come want and loss, whereas the Prophet Elijah is the dispenser of peace and life. When this force for life and peace reigns in the world, laughter is to be found in those creatures doomed to howls and moans.' Besides, the same was true of Balaam's ass: coming on the Angel standing in the middle of road, drawn sword in hand, the ass turned aside into the fields, but Balaam, blind to this vision, beat the ass whose eyes were open.

Was the dog laughing? The idea made him smile, and so it was that he came out into the square in front of the town hall, his face all bright and cheerful.

At the corner of the town hall, the Maharal kept timeless watch, the young bedraggled nymph desperately clinging to his side. The old sage and the beautiful nymph stood covered in snow in the recess of their alcove whose cupola was reminiscent of the fluted concave valve of large sea-shell. Haloed with snow and an ochre-white, slightly sulphurous brightness, they looked more than ever like fluvial or oceanic figures. They emerged from a deep watery darkness – not that which precedes the dawn of the world, nor that at its end, but the darkness, perhaps, that gave birth to the new morning of the world when the flood waters retreated. Morning of second light that broke not long into the course of history, but was already over. Morning of intimacy, when the covenant was renewed and the order of the world redefined. 'For surely your blood of your lives will I require; at the hand of every beast will I require it, and at the hand of man; at the hand of every man's brother will I require the life of man.'

Was it this life of man, so often robbed, scorned, violated by man, that the Maharal talked of in secret with the Emperor Rudolph on that distant Sunday of the year 1492? And Brum, was he now in the company of those two men? Was he now at last party to their discussion?

As he contemplated the statue and thought of Brum, he suddenly became aware of a detail he had never noticed before. Huddled at the Maharal's feet, a counterpart to the young naked girl, was a dog. Was it the one mentioned in 'The Fifth Well', that the sculptor Saloun portrayed here?

It did not seem to be laughing, this strangely crouched dog with thin flanks. No more than it seemed to be howling or moaning. A pensive, hesitant dog. But how could the dog have decided one way or the other, since life and peace, which are to be greeted with laughter, coexist with the approach of death, which ought to be met with a long drawn-out howl?

Bearing within his body close on a century of wisdom and luminous faith, his heart imbued with peace and radiating life, was not the Maharal threatened with death, which the young girl innocently brought to him? The young girl, as beautiful and fragile in her nudity as the famous rose whose scent exuded death. That was why the dog could not make up its mind: cowering in the folds of his master's coat, he was equally sensitive to the old man's strength and serenity and youthful death's sickly smell.

An idea suddenly occurred to Ludvik. He took out of his pocket the book returned to him by Brum after thirty years' reading, extracted from it the collage postcard, folded it vertically, and climbing on to the plinth, he stuck it in the Maharal's raised hand – the one defending itself against the pernicious embrace of death.

'There,' he said, he too clinging to the old man's shoulder, 'the farewell message has become a greeting and a never-ending invitation to a journey. Good luck on your journey, Joachym Brum, on the immense highway of souls!' Then he climbed down, slipped and tumbled at the bottom of the plinth. He found himself flat on his back on the ice-cold paving stones. 'Just like fat Ludmilla!' he thought, and burst out laughing.

He himself was the dog, the humble animal with a good nose, but with no comprehension of the unexpected miracle. Yet, a man until now so confused in his thoughts, so trammelled by his doubting intelligence, he was at that moment perfectly conscious of a rush of pure joy in knowing himself to be alive, supremely at peace. And he laughed and laughed, sitting on his backside on those paving stones dripping with melted snow. He finally got to his feet, brushed down his raincoat, came back towards the statue, stroked the stone dog's head, then walked away. All around him was a world waiting to be discovered, to be questioned, a living, enduring world.

Also available by Sylvie Germain

The Book of Nights

Night of Amber

Days of Anger

The Medusa Child

The Weeping Woman on the Streets of Prague

Infinite Possibilities

The Book of Tobias